D0355501

THE ELECTRICAL EXPERIENCE

THE
ELECTRICAL
EXPERIENCE

a discontinuous narrative

Frank
MOORHOUSE

ANGUS & ROBERTSON PUBLISHERS

ANGUS & ROBERTSON PUBLISHERS
London • Sydney • Melbourne • Singapore
Manila

First published by Angus & Robertson Publishers, Australia, 1974

This revised Arkon paperback edition 1980

National Library of Australia
card number and ISBN 0 207 14107 X

PRINTED IN AUSTRALIA BY HEDGES & BELL PTY LTD

Narratives

•

Fragments

•

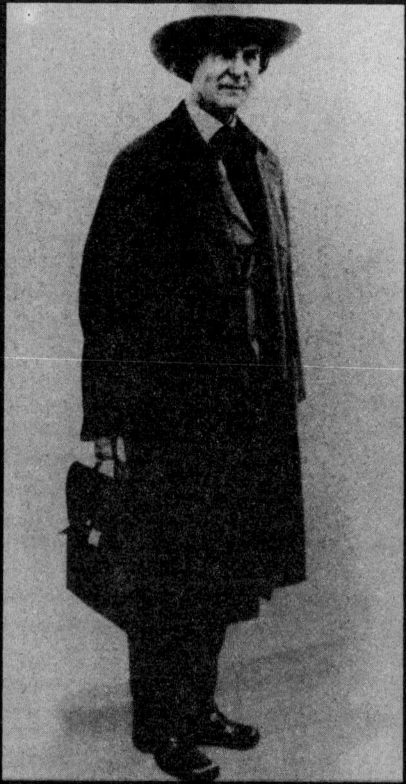

A
Black, Black
Birth

SHE was nurtured in the good fellowship and the ethics of this home, T. George McDowell said to the American who was sitting in the lounge-room staring into his drink.

In this very lounge-room.

They had played draughts, Terri and he.

In 1939, when she was born, you were known as a person. If you wanted something done you knew who to see, if someone said they would do something it got done, you knew who you were dealing with and they knew you, and if you had something on your mind you said it. The street was filled with faces you knew—Bishops, Youngs, Millers, Ferriers, Watts. A dentist surgery with a painted window. Why, at least the dentist surgery still smelled the same. He knew the name of that smell. He remembered it from a talk given to Rotary just after the war. He knew the name of that smell if only he could bring it to mind. The telephone was partly to blame. Before the war you could always get to see the boss of the show and not some underling. Now people didn't go out to see the problem for themselves, they "got on the telephone".

The Bohemian Problem had enveloped his own daughter, Terri. These people who put themselves apart. It was nothing new. He remembered a case about the time she was born. A case of a farm-hand who'd been caught smoking opium under a gum-tree. Near Huskisson. Not a Chinese, an Australian. There was talk also about Old Scribner, a poet of sorts, an educated man, talk about him and opium. But they were people who'd given up. He did not have a solution to the Bohemian Problem. Did this American here in the lounge-room know something about it?

Terri, even as a child, had a will of her own. They hadn't put her birth in the paper. It was considered unwise to put birth notices in the newspaper. That unsavoury interest in whether the child had been conceived in wedlock. Not that there could have been any doubt with Thelma and he, married fifteen years. But you couldn't win. There was talk, suggestion and gossip that it had been a "mistake". Thelma and he had planned to have three children and that was that. Some said that gypsies passing through a town would look to see if there were new births in the newspaper and then steal the child. He gave that no credence.

The temperature was 105. Black Saturday. The sky turned black. The sun could not be properly seen. There was something unnaturally fearful about losing sight of the sun. Some were saying the town would be burned. Some mentioned the end of the world. Villages along the coast disappeared in smoke and flame. Burnt leaves dropped from the sky. The bay was black with burnt ash and the water could not be seen. A scorching wind drove the flames—like frightened horses. He endeavoured to put a stop to talk about the end of the world. Oh, that heat.

It was like looking into a furnace. The town was open to draught, a city is not. He was no city man. He went to the city only on business. On the other hand he was not a village man. A place like Tomerong was not for him. A post-office, store and COR plus Ethyl bowser—one of the first bowsers along that stretch. You had to find the right-size place for the size of man you were.

He told the American about his own first visit to the States, to the St Louis Rotary Convention back in 1923.

"How is it I can remember the address of the St Louis Coliseum from 1923, but I forget the name of someone I met ten minutes ago? Why is that?"

"It is an often remarked characteristic of later years, sir."

This American was a likeable chap.

Some said America was the greatest nation the world had known. He'd heard a fellow refute that. The USA didn't have the largest population—China did. It didn't have the biggest navy, England did. It didn't have the biggest army, France did. It wasn't the healthiest nation, Sweden was. Russia produced more wheat. Germany produced more steel. The Swiss were more democratic. Australia had the best sportsmen. South Africa had more gold. And the United States could not claim to be the most moral nation, with its gangsters.

Still, that was all a long time back. That was what they were saying before the war.

He had a lot of time for the Americans.

When she was born, the town was ringed with fire. He gave a dozen boxes of soft drinks from the factory to the fire-fighters. A public-address system on the back of a van cried out a crackled appeal from the Mayor for volunteers.

A drifter was burned to death near Jerry Bailey. His body was so charred they couldn't lift it. In the heat and sweat of it all he said, damn it, let's put the bones in a box and bury it. They buried the bones virtually on the spot. No one said anything about it. Yalwal was burned to the ground. The townfolk of Yalwal spent a day standing full-clothed in the creek. They stood in the creek up to their necks, singing from a songster, flames all around them. Someone found the songster in their pocket and thought singing was a good idea. Both sides of the creek were ablaze.

A post-office savings bank burned down, and the safe cracked open in the heat. Money was burned. Money sweated and laboured for disappeared in ash. It was like flesh and blood burning. No one could get near the post-office for the heat.

A relief party consisting of Eric McElphone, the coroner, Dr Trenbow, Nurse Denison, and the Harvey Brothers, two of the strongest men in the district, drove three motor-cars to save outlying farmers.

Ted Henson took his horse with him into a creek, and the heat of the burning bush scorched the leather of the saddle. The flames were a hundred feet high. The green leaves burned like paper.

The hooves of the cows fell off from the scorching. Cedric Binks lay face down in a cave and almost suffocated because the fire drew the oxygen from the cave.

The town stopped work to fight the fire.

He visited Thelma that evening in the hospital, taking with him their electric fan for her personal use.

It was almost as though the day had affected Terri, the newborn baby. Perhaps the roaring noise of the fire, the smell of burning eucalyptus and the fear surrounding her, disturbed her for ever.

He saw the Thompson home burn to the ground and it had made ice in his blood and broken his breathing.

The cement washtubs always survived. He saw the burnt de-luxe ice-chest, the porcelain lining cracked by heat. The sight and smell of burned clothes unsettled him, but he couldn't stop himself staring. There was no water, there was nothing that could be done. It was as though the occupant's personal odour was being let loose instead of being kept privately within the four walls of a house. Burned personal things. Things saved, half saved, dragged burning from the house, now smouldering. The paved path leading nowhere. The laid-out garden edged with house bricks. A tap upright in the garden.

A family burned out and exposed.

He'd given to the fund. He couldn't recall how much. Was it £5?

Birds fell from the sky. Magpies, peewees, parrots, fell dead from the sky.

Fire and water gave no mercy.

The town had three enemies: fire: water: the city.

City interests had always worked against the country town. Somehow people had forgotten proper respect for fire and water these days.

A difficult birth. The sky was black. He drank a lot of cordial that day. Everyone did. He was left with no stocks.

The freedom to buy and sell. The freedom to make what you wanted and to sell as you saw fit. The people who could take raw, unshapen material from the earth and organize it into something of value were a special kind of person. He had always been proud to be that kind of person. He was a producer who made other people's skills go to work. He did not do it for wealth. He was not a flashy dresser. Did not own a racehorse or a seaside cottage. Unlike Curlewis, who, anyhow, had inherited. He had the capital if he wanted that style of life, but that was not what he considered the purpose of business.

The policeman's widow had been speeding along the highway through a tunnel of flames in her Essex and had struck a fallen tree. The branch, still burning, had pierced

6

her heart. It had passed through her left breast, through the nipple, into her heart, still burning until extinguished by her blood. So the men who found her said. One told Backhouse at the newspaper about it. She was pinned to the seat of the Essex. They pulled her off the seat and carried her to the car with the branch through her heart.

He regretted his association with her. As a young widow she had not been popular. Young widows are never popular with the married women. She had been on her way out of the town for good—the Essex contained all her possessions. She had told no one she was leaving.

People leaving like that sometimes meant the end of a town. You never quite knew deep down whether a town would go ahead. You looked a town over and decided to settle. He never rented. He always built. It was an act of faith in one's own good judgement about the town.

You never really knew whether a town would go ahead or go back. He'd seen a town die.

He'd seen them one by one pull out of a town as he was growing up. The hardware store closed, the baker left, the barber. His childhood friends disappeared overnight.

It chilled his very being.

Only last week he stood looking at the salesyard, disused for thirty years, the rusted reservoir. What was left of the blacksmith's shop. The anvil was still there. The forge. They just walked out at the end. Boarded-up, deserted houses. Rubbish of people who lived there thirty, forty years ago. The hotel burned down probably for insurance. You could see where the life of the town had flown. Like a moving picture suddenly stopped. The people became an old photograph. They had walked along the wooden plank verandas, which served as a footpath. All weathering and rotting back into the soil.

He remembered chasing his childhood friends along the street. There'd been bargaining and buying. People danced at the Memorial Hall. The floor now fallen out. Billy Ryan laid that floor.

There'd been committees and they'd planned improvements to the town. Signs had been put up, some still standing, unheeded, no people behind the words.

One man could hold a town. You had to watch. One day you might find that people were privately selling out. Others began leaving overnight, bills unpaid. Farewell functions for government people became more frequent and they were not replaced.

His childhood friends disappeared overnight.

The policeman's widow had left without a word.

But this town was solid.

Terri could have stayed in the town, instead she chose a life of disorder. People kept an eye on each other in the town. Now she was in the city being looked after by a psychiatrist. Perhaps the city was not her size.

When a business fell, it shook the town. But you had to look to see if it was bad management or the town that was at fault.

Like the ice-making business. It used to be one of the biggest in town. Refrigeration put an end to that. He always said it was one business where the raw material was free.

He thanked god for refrigeration. It made this country bearable. And carbonated soft drinks which he brought to the town. Although it was his business he still delighted in the powerful fizzing coldness of a good soft drink as it hit the mouth and tongue. Made you know you had a mouth that could *feel*.

And the milk-"shake". He'd introduced that to the coast too. It was good for the coast. The Milky Way. Ayrshires, Jerseys, Friesians, Illawarra Shorthorns, Guernseys. He had grown up on a dairy farm farther down the coast. He was a town man but not ashamed to have been a dairy farmer's son.

The South Coast produced a better sort of person. Quicker to take to new techniques, quick to understand technical matters. A technical type of person. Independent of the city. Fishermen, farmers, and business men. Not having the railway helped. Kept the coast separate. Made it what it was. He'd said this many times. Made them rely on each other. It helped people to be separated from the city and all its Public Servants and Unions. He liked Kangaroo Valley farther up the coast.

They were a separate people and better for it.

But he was a town man.

This American chap seemed a decent sort of fellow.

The American knew his daughter Terri up in the city. She had left the town and her family, gone her own way.

"There is high authority," he said to the American, "for the proposition that a child owes no natural affection to the parent. . . ."

The city sapped the towns of the young.

"She would, as a child, ask herself questions and give herself answers."

You never knew, perhaps the heat of the day of her birth had something to do with her personality, had scorched her. Seared her.

"Where then," he asked the American, "do you find Peace of Mind? Rotary does not pretend to solve the Great Mysteries, but it teaches how to organize life and give it a System. It has taken rules from many places and welded them into a creed and a code."

T. George McDowell paused, considered, and said, "But I do not care for words in top hats. I believe in shirt-sleeve words. I believe in getting the job done. We're like that on the coast. We believe in the right technique and the right machine."

And the Right Frame of Mind. The Right Frame of Mind could be brought about. The ability to smile and keep on smiling had a lot to do with it.

There was a Chinese proverb: "A man without smile should not open shop."

He and Thelma left the lights burning in the house porch at night as a way of smiling to the world.

"We're all mechanics on the South Coast. Not like out West or up the North Coast. We're not slow to change or to see the next move. We're all mechanically minded and Systematic."

He'd liked talking with this American.

Life's experience had taught him that never once had speaking to a stranger been anything but to his advantage. Although inherently shy as a young man, he had learned early to talk to someone as if they owed you money. In all his life, including his world travel, the only person with whom he had been unable to converse in good fellowship was his daughter Terri, and this was a source of some distress to both him and Thelma.

"The Greeks believed there was a time in the past when things were easier.

"The scientifically minded person believes that there will be time in future when things will be easier."

From a Speech by T. George McDowell

GEORGE McDOWELL DOES THE JOB

HE assessed himself as "up to the date". Perhaps in his thinking he was already one calendar ahead—perhaps already into 1939. Anyhow, quite a modern man. He was fortunate too in having a wife who shared his Life Plan—a situation which, in his case, meant that his capacity was doubled rather than halved as in sharing, say, a cake.

He often said that if it wasn't for Thelma he would not be where he was today, although he was a self-made man (but not one who worshipped his maker). She had, though, worked for him in the business without wages during the early times and more recently during the economic depression. She was far more diligent at bottle inspection than the average bottle-washer. Like all cordial-makers he lived in a nightmare that one day a bottle would slip through inspection and poison a customer.

So therefore, although he and she did not go about the town propounding it in conversation, as up to the date people they believed and practised family planning through birth "control". His wife was also a practising Anglican. He was, well, put him down as one who served his fellow man, a business man, and a Rotarian.

To have a family plan went with having a life plan. Nothing could be accomplished without a Blueprint.

Together, of course, with initiative and capital.

They had two well-spaced children and intended having one more to bring the number to "three". "Three" seemed to him to be a manageable and modern number, although they had both themselves come from large families. His wife had been fitted with a diaphragm by a city physician, but she asked that he also wear a condom "just in case", and he did. He himself was a precautionary man, although it was true that all business did involve risk-taking. He had never said this to Thelma, but he felt that somehow the time when they were trying for a child, as it were, was made somehow tingling for them, because on these occasions they did not use, of course, any—precaution. He supposed it was because then, as it were, his "skin" touched her flesh, the flesh, that is, inside her.

15

George McDowell cleared a tickle from his mental throat.

They were, certainly, the times most vividly recalled. Intercourse, he realized in maturity, was not everything it was cracked up to be. They had not let it become a "complex". His wife, he sometimes thought, was herself not a highly sexed woman, and although he became quite aroused at times, he was not overly preoccupied, he hoped. He had exercised self-control, as harsh as it was on her, in regard to the policeman's widow. He observed that the limitations and restrictions on the matter of sexual indulgence, placed by Thelma in their marriage, sometimes aroused him, her unwillingness, he had perhaps that sort of personality which was, which savoured, well, the restraint she imposed, the limitations on when, and her refusals. And now and then, though rarely, he imposed himself on her, and the silent, wordless, impositions he enjoyed too. It had to do, he speculated, with the basic economic principle of scarcity. Though really, this aspect of their lives he did not truly understand and did not ponder over much and which was not to say, either, that they did not conduct their married life *correctly*.

She insisted that the condom be flushed down the lavatory immediately after, and that he wash.

She did not, quite properly, want the girls finding them around the place or to step out in the morning to be confronted by it.

He badly wanted a son.

"I think we should have, that it is really time for us to consider having, another child if you still want for us to have a third."

She said it as they prepared for bed. He was brushing his teeth with Kolynos dental cream and going over in his mind a masonic catechism he needed to know for Tuesday's Lodge. He did not know why he kept it up. He continued brushing, knowing what she meant and feeling in his pubic region that instant stirring. He smiled boyishly at her but she did not smile. Perhaps the toothpaste around his mouth, and he removed the smile, changed his voice to a proper tone, and said, yes, he would like another child to bring it up to "three", spitting into the white porcelain basin.

He went to bed without his pyjama trousers and without precaution.

After, because of germ life, they usually washed, she first, and he second, but because they were trying for a child she did not douche. When he returned from washing, she said to him, "People will think I'm awfully old to be having another child."

"You're older than customary, I suppose."

"Forty is really quite old. To be having a child."

"We've always said we'd have three," he said firmly, referring to their plan.

"After this birth I think I should perhaps have an operation."

"*Shusssh*—don't talk that way," he said, holding her Herco-smelling hand, squeezing it, not liking the clamminess of the idea of a surgical operation on that area of the body. He himself had had no sickness in his adult life to talk of.

But thinking also that at the same time it would mean an end to birth-control devices, although, on the other hand, a feeling that she would then be simply, well, a hollow body— and maybe of no interest at all.

He thought then about the Group Scout Meeting that would be held later that week. The plans for the camp up at Mt Keira and the log cabin they were building. Some were in favour of a rustic way of doing the window frames, while he himself preferred a tradesmanlike job all round. He would argue that. No one preferred rusticity when it leaked.

Head on pillow looking up at the new plaster egg-and-dart cornice there in the dark of their new bedroom of their new house, the curtain lace lapping against the window and the breeze slightly bumping the blind cord, lying there he concluded that as far as he could see, everything in his life was being correctly done.

He was being recognized. He was becoming a person-about-the-town.

The new house was finished in detail right down to the built-in holder for toilet-paper rolls, and furnished with a number of electrically operated appliances and a new Stromberg Carlson which only gave static during storms.

He had been elected District Scout Master. In his speech he had said that the supreme challenge of each generation was "holding" the next generation. Keeping control of the young. That it was possible for a generation to be "lost", for control to slip and for civilization to be without a generation to take over. He referred to the twenties in America, where a whole generation had been "lost". Maybe the law of oak inheres in oak, he'd said; nevertheless, while membership of a family can ensure that the values of that family inhere in the children of that family, Community Organizations had to police this and to ensure that "replacement parts" were available for those families lacking values. Community Organizations had to give these children replacement values.

He was outspoken in the Chamber of Commerce but was keeping an open mind on tourism. On one hand the tourist spent in the town—on his soft drinks, he was pleased to say—yet he could concede that they depreciated local facilities and roads without paying rates. He was able, he hoped, to place his own personal advantage aside when considering community issues.

He had reluctantly joined the Sequicentenary Committee, reluctantly, because he felt the country areas had not received the sort of subsidy needed. He suspected it was someone in the city with a big idea for getting themselves knighted, and that the country towns were expected to obey. The city was beginning to look upon the towns as retinue.

He had refused a donation to the Roman Catholic School Fund because he did not believe in such schools separate from the public schools. Schools should, he thought, mirror the community in all its diversity—the rich, the poor, the bright, the dull, the protestant, the Roman Catholic. This way the child was prepared for the sort of community which lay ahead for him. Education occurred in the playground. One day this division between Roman Catholic and the rest would lead to bloodshed in this country. They had made the division themselves. He hoped, of course, it could be avoided.

They owed allegiance to an authority outside this country.

He had moved a motion at the A and H Society to refuse gypsies admission to the showground.

Gypsies.

He had a morbid feeling about the gypsies. He stopped once when they flagged him down, parked on the roadside in their American Buicks. A rather pretty gypsy girl just out of childhood, her hair half covering her dark face, and close up he could not judge her age—thirteen?—had flagged him down. Gypsy girl. Had smiled at him in a certain way. He rather thought, self-control slipping, that . . . maybe . . . the gypsy girl . . . would . . . he had lost his self-control for that instant, she called her mother, his hand on her arm, she had called her mother, groin against her, she called her mother, and the mother was morbidly attractive too, aroused in his trousers, he wanted to offer money to lie down in the bushes with the gypsy girl . . . maybe an arrangement, but he could go no further than £1. They wanted, instead, to tell his fortune.

Really, he thought, pulling himself together, he had thought really they were broken-down, needing assistance. The mother asked him to take everything from his pocket to tell his fortune, his handkerchief, his keys, his penknife, his loose change, his wallet, of course, yes, of course, to tell his fortune. She asked for the silver and he gave it to her. Instructed him to do it, and he felt rather hot and helpless. She asked for his hand, of course, he held out his hand. For the telling of his fortune. He tried to look for the young gypsy girl. For the telling of the fortune. The coming of a female figure, a child, a female dark and of a troubled nature. Thoughts of suicide. He looked for the young dark gypsy girl. Other girls in the back of the black Buicks. He had a hand which held money, through which the light did not shine.

He became uncertain, it seemed to be getting dark, where were his possessions, who was at the car? He could not see the young, alluring gypsy girl. The older gypsy had the things from his pocket. He was prepared for her to have the silver. He wanted his things back.

"I'm sorry, I would like my things back, please return my

things."

She asked for £1 note for the telling of the fortune. He grabbed and took back his things, backing towards his car, she held things to him withdrawing them when he went to snatch.

"Take the change, the silver."

He had his wallet, she took a £1, she was putting it in her bosom.

"I thought you needed help or something. Take the silver."

She kept mumbling and coming towards him and being close to him, and it seemed to be growing quickly dark.

Sweating cold, he clambered into his Ford. He drove fast but stopped a mile or so along to check his things and found £2 missing from his wallet. How she'd taken it, he did not know. He saw no way of returning to them and getting his money back. He'd been a damn' fool. Then he noticed that his new horn, which barked like a dog for moving cattle off the road, was also gone.

He ran out of petrol at Jaspers Brush. They had milked his tank.

He did not mention the stopping for the gypsies, the loss of the money, the horn, or the milking of the tank, to Thelma. Or anyone else.

The little dark-eyed gypsy girl.

"Again?" his wife queried, as he rubbed himself against her.

"I feel like it again," he whispered.

"All right," she said, moving apart her legs. "It's not like you."

He had moved that the gypsies not be permitted to enter the showground at showtime, for the purposes of fortune-telling.

He had never been bitten by a snake. He had always taken the snake-bite as a mark of carelessness in a man.

Fred Watts had been bitten by a snake only last week and in delirium saw all his old friends, some dead for forty years, and some he'd seen only the day before up at the Adelong Races, saw them all marching in file past his eyes, down into a black cavern. They had turned their eyes neither to the right nor to the left, and gave no sign of having seen him. They were dressed in the suits and hats of their times, some in the dress of forty years ago and some in the dress of today. Every person he had known in his life passed before his eyes.

Fred had treated himself with nicotine, which was useless. Fred was, and always would be, slapdash.

George McDowell, without conceit, concluded that his personal book-keeping was in order.

Yes.

He had heard the arguments against planning of the family. That it did not build the nation. That the yellow and black peoples of the world would soon outnumber the whites. He believed that birth control should not be used for avoiding family responsibility. He believed each parent should have one child and that a third should be for the building of the nation. That seemed to be a scientific and modern number.

"You haven't been to the bathroom," his wife murmured.

She meant after the second time.

Tiredly he got up, feet swinging into his slippers, and went to the bathroom to wash himself.

Love of luxury and not birth control he blamed for the decline of the British stock. The line between comfort and luxury had to be drawn. Comfort was the justified basic wage for hard effort. Luxury was excessive self-reward—over-paying. Hot water, refrigeration and electrically operated appliances, were the New Servants and he did not consider these luxury. They were necessary for the recharging of the body's energies.

He believed in Modernization. What did the job best. Birth "control" seemed to him to be a good example of the modernization of married life. Good business kept the community up to the date in its commodities. Good tradesmen kept up to the date with new materials and methods and cleaned up after the job.

George McDowell smiled, there in the bathroom: smiled at himself in the mirror on the cabinet door; a tentative, uncharacteristic smile of a distantly related, unofficial self: not the sort of humour he cared for, because, although one should be capable of laughing at oneself, one should not laugh at one's values and ideals: but, nevertheless, he smiled as these words formed in his head, "You are a good tradesman, George, and you clean up after the job."

The words and the smile were then expunged from his mind, leaving behind no trace or residue of self-mockery.

Colouring Electric-light Globes

•

Around the time of the Sesquicentenary George put this in the
local paper, but very few took the trouble.

**"For a festive occasion dip electric-light globes in a mixture of
sodium silicate and gelatin, coloured by water-soluble dyes. The
thickness of the mixture is a matter of experimentation."**

The Song of the Cream

•

"Let's sing a song of the cream,
Through vats and pasteur systems,
Whose polished linings gleam,
To a slowly turning wooden churn,
Flows now the chastened cream."

A Piece of South Coast Verse, 1938

GEORGE McDOWELL CHANGES NAMES

O N 9th July 1938, when George McDowell strode home
from business that evening to eat his tea before going
to a meeting, his wife, leaning back from the rise of
steam while straining the beans, told him that she was expecting their third child.

He kissed her on the cheek, she averting her eyes from the
beans as a gesture of appreciation for the kiss and to separate
the announcement from her task of straining the beans.

"In or about February," she said.

"It will be hot in hospital," he said, frowning at the bad
planning.

"Doctor says to expect a somewhat difficult birth because
of my age."

"Forty isn't that old," he said, himself being thirty-five.

"For having children, the medical profession seem to think
so. I told him that three was our plan."

He washed his hands in the bathroom with Solvol.

Of course it meant the training of another child. The
training of a child had always been heart-racking. He did not
relish the punishment of children, the beatings, the smackings,
the sobbings, the locking of children in the broom closet.
There was always, too, what seemed to him to be the unnecessary messiness and untidiness of untrained children
which remained for him a puzzle of nature.

He was pondering also the coincidence that on the day his
wife should be pronounced pregnant, he should change his
name.

As they sat down at the dining-room table, the girls prim
and quiet, serviettes under chin, "The Lord make us Truly
Grateful", his wife asked, "At work today, dear, anything
of interest?"

"Yes, as a matter of fact," he said, twinkling, glad at last
to be asked, having waited for what seemed a correct and
decorous length of time and distance from his wife's announcement of the coming of the child, "I changed my name today,"
he announced, lightheartedly.

"How do you mean?" she said, moving fruit in the fruit
basket, a way she had of making herself steady, by being busy.

The children looked towards him with wide, unsure eyes.

"How do you mean, father?"

"I'll show you," he said, and, leaving the table, he went to the sideboard, failing to find paper, he went then to the telephone table.

He returned with a pad and indelible pencil.

With a flourish, determined but not yet habit, he wrote, "T. George McDowell." He licked the pencil and wrote in indelible purple, "T. George McDowell."

"It's longer" was the first thing his wife said, staring at the new signature, pushed across to her on the pad headed Messages.

The children peered across.

"Why, daddy?"

"What does T stand for?" the older daughter, Gwen asked.

"T stands for Terence, daddy's other Christian name," Thelma told the children.

He went on eating, looking not at the food but at the new signature.

"Why don't you use it if it comes first?" Gwen asked.

"A long story," T. George McDowell said, returning in a flash and a spin to a boy with a leather schoolbag monogrammed TMCD with a red-hot piece of wire, riding a pony to a one-room coastal school, a drawing illustrating all the people of the Empire by children in different colours and national dress, all smiling, toothily, the enterprising spirit of the Anglo-Saxon race. "At my school, you see, we had two Terence McDowells, and I being the younger had to use my second name. As so often happens, it stuck."

He never quite overcame that bewilderment and displacement of having met, so early in his life, among such a small group, someone of the same name.

"Why have you changed your signature now? And what about the bank and so on?" Thelma asked unsurely.

"For emphasis," he said. "It has more oomph."

He had wanted to change his name to T. George since 1923, when he attended the St Louis Rotary Convention, an event which charged his life with zeal and which had begun

28

him on his realization of his System for Success. But only now, some many years later, did he feel established enough in the town to, well, "get away with it".

"T. George McDowell," his wife said in a low voice. "T. George McDowell."

"It will help, I think," T. George said, "especially in my dealings with the city and when we travel."

"Does it change our names too, daddy?" asked the younger.

"I expect the locals will give you a bit of good-natured fun about it."

"I suppose so. I took it down to the printery today to have the new letterhead set up. Backhouse said it looked 'Americanized'."

Backhouse saying that pleased him, although one didn't know about Backhouse. Backhouse held himself off, was inclined to make remarks which meant more to himself than to the person addressed.

"Yes, it does," his wife said, saying T. George McDowell over in a low voice, as if trying to recognize the name.

"I've noticed in Rotary that many of the Rotarians from the city have adopted the use of their initial."

He masticated a mouthful of food. The family waited for him to go on.

As if they were waiting for yet further explanation.

"It makes you stand out from the herd. That is the theory of it. In business," he said, beginning what sounded like a speech, "it pays to have something which catches the eye—makes them remember you next time."

He patted his mouth with the white serviette, leaving a beetroot stain.

"A lot of the fun that is poked is at those who dare to be different. It is a way of getting people back into the common lot. There is nothing most like better than to pull a person back," he told the girls and Thelma.

"The lowest common denominator," his wife agreed.

"I see where Australia is producing its own tacks and wireless valves," he said, opening the newspaper, changing the subject modestly.

"Don't read at the table, dear. It's a bad example for the girls."

Pouring the tea from the traymobile, Thelma said, "I expect at the long weekend we'll have quite an exodus from the city coming through."

"Boiled radiators and punctured tyres. Should sell plenty of drinks. We'll be working back to build up stocks."

"It's such a messy way of spending a weekend. Nowhere to wash properly."

"Can we go camping, mummy?"

"When you become a girl guide and learn to camp properly," Thelma replied, "that is more than half the trouble. They come from the city and have not been trained to camp."

"Harry Fox is grumbling that the tourists camp in his paddocks. But some of the more tourist-minded in the Chamber want the farmers to let them camp."

He found he had picked up the newspaper again and Thelma took it away putting it out of reach, and then said to the girls, "You must not talk to strangers."

"I gave a young fellow a lift today."

"Oh yes."

"He was dressed in black. I asked him about it and he told me it was a German-style uniform. It was a black uniform which he got while in Germany himself. Black shirt, black trousers, black leather knee-boots. You couldn't miss him. He stood out beside the road."

"Was he German?"

"No, Australian."

"I don't know what to think of that business over there."

"All you can say is that he's getting the place into shape. But he cannot last. Dictators do not last. No man who doesn't smile can last long in any public position. I never have seen a photograph of Adolf Hitler smiling."

He had once, at a sideshow in 1919, been tempted by a gypsy to be hypnotized but could not submerge himself. He wanted to go and be hypnotized but could not hand his will over to another. He stood fixed in the sawdust outside the sideshow tent as she coaxed him, staring straight into his eyes, there in the crowd, saying, "Come on, young man, venture into the dark beyond, you will become my slave."

He'd felt sickly weak, drawn, but wouldn't give his feet the instruction to go. His mind said no, but his whole physical yearning was to go and give himself over to her.

He was an individualist. A student of electricity and magnetism even then, a scientifically minded person and would not give himself over to hocus-pocus.

About the German thing, he saw the appeal of the torchlight and the singing and the wearing of national uniforms and leather knee-boots. It would be good for a country to march and sing together in a surge of unity. As opposed to all the political backbiting and squabbling. But no he was an individualist.

He had stared at the man in black uniform but found that he was not a Nazi but an adventurer, and his nervous curiosity about the Nazis was then deflated. One heard so much.

"Was he pleasant?"

"A little strange."

The man in the black uniform told him stories of midnight raids and the searching of Jewish women. Of the German secret police who made women strip, forced the women to be their whores, to clean and polish their boots with their mouths, lips and then to crouch naked and polish them with their pubic region.

"Hadn't you better leave for the meeting?" Thelma reminded him.

"Yes," he murmured and told the girls to help their mother.

He would try out the new name on those at the meeting, although he didn't feel in the mood to have his leg pulled.

He remembered that the child was expected and before he left, after putting on the armour of his best suit, he went to the kitchen and kissed his wife again on the cheek.

"I almost forgot—I'm glad about the planned child."

His wife smiled, pleasantly, and said, "It had gone completely out of my mind for the time being."

Tractor Anecdote

•

Backward North Coast tenant farmer to tractor salesman:
When you boys can make a tractor that can have a foal to take
its place when it's worn out, then I'll be interested.

Salesman: Ah, but the tractor doesn't eat when it's not working.

BUSINESS NO PICNIC

I N 1929 George McDowell went to the Highlands for a weekend to examine his life and to try to get the cafés to start taking bottled soft drinks. Married one year, his cordial factory was making a profit, but other problems, however, hovered. He had not really mastered shyness, for instance, although his Powers of Concentration had improved, he thought.

Apart from questions of personality and philosophy of life, there was the world. The economic crisis looming, though few seemed to believe it, and the implications of electricity now that the town supply had been switched on, though most ignored that too, except to debate whether the street lights should stay on all night or be turned off at midnight.

His cordial factory was linked to the town electricity, one of the first. His trouble was not electricity but the town water. It needed triple filtration. Competition from Nowra or the city could hurt him especially if they extended the rail past Nowra. But he did not fear competition, he reminded himself. He believed that when it came to foodstuffs, people would buy only from someone they knew. His living presence on the coast was a guarantee.

His car boiled and while waiting for it to cool, he sat on the running-board, made a cup of tea from the boiling radiator, and ate Thelma's tomato sandwiches.

When he reached the town, the guest-house, Wychwoode, seemed oddly quiet.

At the sound of the car James Coffey, owner, in plus-fours, war-limp, came down to get the bags, his cigar plugged in his mouth. George always thought to himself that the cigar in Coffey's mouth always promised more than there was.

"Wonderful to see you, George. Bad news though—but, anyhow, how are you?—domestic staff, would you believe it, are on a strike. On a strike."

Coffey took both bags. "Here let me—that's what a guest-house is all about."

Strike?

George didn't feel right that the older man should carry

35

his bags, but he took it as a tribute to his rising in the business world so young.

"Do?" said Coffey. "What can I do? Nothing." Coffey made it sound like action and decision.

George remained impassive towards his fellow business man as they climbed the stairs and said nothing suggesting endorsement of Coffey's inaction. He had learned only recently that an impassive appearance could be used to lead the other person to say more, to go further than they wanted, to reveal—usually their weakness. Coffey went on firmly about there being nothing that could be done. He did not like Coffey's confidence of defeat.

Cigar or not.

The guest-house had electricity, but although the main light in his room worked, the bed lamp did not. Typical. George carried his own globe because hotels used weak globes to save money.

George braked the Chev too severely and stalled it, so impatient was his movement, so determined was he to sustain his impulse. To get things moving.

People who rely on inertia, he believed, are easy prey to a man of action. A person who made a move stood a high chance of success. There were so few who did. Most people waited for things to happen *to* them.

Mrs K, the housekeeper at Wychwoode, sat in her tidy house with her hands crossed tidily on her lap.

"You can't strike against your own town. That's what you're doing. A place of work is like the family—pride and loyalty are owed," he told her, pacing about her living-room.

"We have," she said, shortly and hopelessly.

"To strike against your employer is to say that he is a dishonest man."

"That's not what we're saying, Mr McDowell. I don't like going on a strike any more than the next person, and this is the very first and only time."

She was outwardly firm, but George sensed her desire to be

back at work, her misgivings, her unease amid an unfamiliar situation.

He played on her desire to be back doing what she knew.

He went on, ". . . why, grown people each sitting at home sulking. Working for each other is our sacred interchange. A town is a co-operative reliance on each other to do his job."

His voice had strength and bluster which spurred him on as he heard himself. He did not know what he was saying at the time, but he knew when it was having effect.

He said things about goodness' sake, Mrs K, you have known James Coffey for how many years and the economic crisis and hard times.

After shaking her head during most of it, she did then get up resignedly and get her things.

"What about the others?" she said with some trepidation. "I'm letting them down."

"I'll worry about the others."

She said, no, she wasn't going, and sat down again, her things on the floor beside her.

George talked on, paced about. "We all live too close for us to be striking against each other. Striking is for those who don't know each other. The city."

She got up again, sat down again, but at last moved towards the door.

"Mind you," she said, "I'm only going back to talk. I'll not do a touch of work until this is settled properly."

Yes, yes.

Finally he got her into the car.

The cook said she'd put up with conditions long enough, and the cook at Bundanoon only worked forty-four hours and no broken shifts.

"Mrs K is out in the car and she's going back to work. She's willing to go back—to keep this in the family of employment. Not to make wounds which might not heal."

Agnes looked out the window to see for herself.

"For heaven's sake, Agnes, you're the last person I would have thought needed looking after by people from the city.

By some Union People you've never seen."

"I suppose if Mrs K is going back . . . but there'll have to be some immediate. . ."

Yes, yes, yes.

Two down.

The others were easy. Mrs K and Agnes in the car did the trick. He blustered them and held the curtain of their front window to show them. His two prisoners-of-war.

"Strike at Wychwoode! This is not the way country people settle things."

"But the Union Man over the telephone said to stay out until he got here."

They'd actually telephoned the city.

"Damn it, do we trust the voice on the telephone now more than the voice of those around us?"

The telephone made things happen too quickly.

Which one of them had the nerve to book a telephone trunk call to the city. That took some nerve.

"Some things," he told them, "are too important for the telephone."

People got things wrong over the telephone because they were too nervous. Many letters answered themselves in a fortnight, he always said.

So they'd actually telephoned the city. Fancy that.

"Who made the call?"

They didn't answer. He looked over his shoulder at them, huddled and glum. He looked at Agnes beside him. No reply. They weren't telling.

The boots, Old Simon, odd-jobman, cow-milker, wouldn't go back to work. He said he had made his decision and he didn't care what the others were doing and no young whipper-snapper was going to tell him what to do. He wouldn't rat on the union.

How had Coffey let things get so bad with his staff?

Whipper-snapper George gave up on Simon, shutting the

weathered door of the weathered shack behind him, full of stuffed parrots and sea trunks. Beer bottles trimmed the edge of the dirt path.

He couldn't believe Simon would have made the trunk-line call to the city. He could not imagine Simon with a telephone in his hand.

He dragged the gate shut. Simon's tethered goat whinnyed at him.

In the car the others were sitting low, probably fearing that old Simon would come out and berate them.

He told them the white lie that Simon wasn't feeling well.

This seemed to hearten them. He sensed that Simon was the backbone of their little nonsense.

He got the Chev into gear and turned around, when Simon came to the door and shouted, "You can all go to bloody hell— ratting on the union."

He revved the car up to block out Simon's voice, waved with mock cheeriness, as if they were great old mates, and shouted back, "Tomorrow—hope you're feeling better." Being on the side nearest Simon, he hoped the others didn't catch what he'd cried out. If they did, they perhaps chose not to show it.

At full throttle the Chev jerked off down the rutted road.

Agnes was even singing as she prepared the evening meal and the others were all seemingly, at least, relieved to be back at work.

They knew how to do their job: they didn't know how to have a strike. No one liked doing unfamiliar things. He'd banked on that.

The few guests who'd stayed, fending for themselves, were relaxing now in the lounge. Coffey was effusive, expansive.

What had Coffey done! Nothing.

He said to Coffey, "The only socialists I've ever known talk about work and the value of work but never do any."

Pleased with himself for having got things going, exhilarated too with having come through a private Shyness Test, he allowed himself a rare glass of stout with Coffey. He had to screw himself tight inside to approach people. To get out from inside took a lot of personal electricity.

"The working people have a puny spirit which is a direct result of lack of self-confidence. They always have to be bolstered up by some agitator. Our task as business men is to offer them superior leadership," he told Coffey.

"This Tea Rooms Award. . . ."

"Every work-place has its own nature—an award never takes heed of that," he told Coffey." One set of conditions cannot be imposed on all. No two enterprises are alike. They're trying to make everyone wear the same clothes."

Coffey nodded, drinking down a whole whisky. George didn't quite know if his words were wasted.

Coffey was no thinker.

"There are two classes—those who are Self-movers and those who have to be coaxed, cajoled, and pushed."

He stopped talking and looked into the empty stout glass. He had drunk that quickly! He refused another.

For heaven's sake, here he was, needing to cajole Coffey—a fellow business man.

Coffey was not quite up to the mark. The burned-out globe, that sort of thing. He played the big fellow about the town. Golfing and so on.

After tea they joined the guests around the pianola and a chap from Bega played the banjo. George excused himself early. Thank god, he thought, for wireless; it'll spare us the amateur musician.

He felt tired right out—a business man was up against it— one man against thousands. One man against the power of the Unions. It was lonely and hard being a small business man. A Problem-solver. A Self-mover against all the obstacles of the world.

Next day, after calling on the two cafés and giving them a sample range of his cordials and some sales talking—although he'd promised Thelma he would take a complete rest—he returned to the guest-house and saw Coffey talking with a stranger in the downstairs hall.

It turned out to be the Union Man from the city, arrived on the midday train.

George noticed he wore riding-boots—from the city and he wore riding-boots.

From the look and sound of it, Coffey was taking a brow-beating.

George joined them, standing hands on hips, eyes to the floor, listening to the Union Man with great impatience.

"And you'll pay them for their holidays," the Union Man said.

George had always found this outrageous. Why should he pay for another man's holiday?

George butted in, "Every business has to arrange its own affairs."

"And who the hell are you?"

George decided not to answer. The Union Man turned to Coffey and said, "Who is this person?"

"This is George McDowell, a business friend."

"George McDowell—by god, I know about you—some sort of damn' soft-drink factory down the coast—my god, yes, I've heard all about you. You keep your nose out of this McDowell."

George was rather pleased that he was known, but did not have a clue for what reason he might be known.

"I'm making this my business," George heard himself say.

"Look, McDowell, go back down the coast and back to your rot-gut lolly-water."

In a second of fury George was about to say, "I'll take you to court", but remembered he was opposed to using the courts in man-to-man situations, and so, instead, he seized the Union Man by the scruff of the neck and seat of the trousers and tried to frog-march him out of the guest-house. They stumbled together into the slow sunlight of the afternoon.

The Union Man freed himself with a twist, caught more by surprise than by George.

Shouting at George, he said something about the Factory Act and being empowered and not to lay a finger.

Coffey limped quickly down the steps, upset, restrained George, muttering, "Trouble enough."

George said, "You better not show yourself around my factory."

The Union Man said that was just what he intended doing and thanked him for the idea.

They stood there in the street, opposed, and out of breath.

"Please," Coffey said, holding George's arm.

Delighted to his heart that he'd thrown the Union Man off the premises but urged away by Coffey, George went off, leaving Coffey in his own mess. Coffey lacked stomach.

George slapped his thigh with exhilaration as he went along the streets in no particular direction, reliving the incident.

Finally he went to the California Café and had a soda with plenty of chipped ice.

He said to Margoulis that enterprise, freedom to our own lives, would be finished if we let inspectors, city Union People and all the rest push us.

Margoulis appeared not quite comprehending, nevertheless agreed, and went on wiping the glasses left by the Saturday matinée interval.

He took the opportunity to point out to Margoulis that with bottled drinks and straws he wouldn't have to wash up the glasses.

But as a gesture of goodwill he admired Margoulis's new soda fountain, refrigerated wells, goose-neck taps.

Riding-boots.

He'd like to see him try.

The remark which hurt the most was the Union Man saying something about him living in the dark ages.

For a go-ahead man, that hurt.

Back in his room at Wychwoode, no sign of the Union Man, he lay on his bed in the late hot afternoon, hands behind his head, and drifted from exhilaration into miserableness.

He had a thought about himself which made him miserable.

It was this: I am a man held in my interlocking restraints: I am not free to enjoy the fruits of pleasure.

Interlocking restraints.

Sometimes his spirit cried out, wept, he wanted sometimes to be, just for one day, indolent. To say, drink alcohol, like some of the others. To lay down the burden. He could see nothing in gambling. But yet there must be something in it for men to pursue it fanatically. That was just another pleasure he could not touch. He was locked in place. In the yoke. He feared the rules. He was frightened that relaxation was irreversible. That, once relaxed, the rules would not return to place. A slide would begin. Into what? What did he fear?

Into insignificance.

He did not want to be insignificant. That was his terror, his nightmare.

Sin wasn't a matter of hellfire for him. Sin was for him misdirected energy, if it was anything.

He really didn't know how to sin.

He was swept with tearfulness, like a rain squall across the sea.

He pulled himself together.

Up again, he washed his face, wetted his hair, parted it, and went downstairs.

The Union Man was definitely gone. Coffey was at golf. That dejected him. He played no sport himself. After throwing a stick to the dog for a while, he decided to go back a night earlier than planned.

Packing the car, he jarred his thumb on the door. He could hardly bear it. He hopped about blowing warm air on his hand, damning and blasting and f-dashing. It hurt like the blazes. It was a bad sign, lack of inner co-ordination.

Driving along with his aching thumb, on his way out of town he pulled up at the railway station, idling there and looking about for the Union Man.

The Union Man was there. Riding-boots and all. George saw him from a distance. He was talking with the station-master. George switched off the ignition and went onto the platform. George then noticed something. He noticed that the Union Man was about his age. He'd really thought him older. And he noticed this also, he saw that the Union Man was clenching and unclenching his hand behind his back as he talked with the station-master.

Why, thought George, this Union Man is a nervous sort.

George watched from the platform entrance. No, I have nothing more to say, and went away without the Union Man seeing him.

We are all shy, observed George wondrously, we are all shy people.

Driving off, his thumb aching as he bumped along the bad mountain road. He admitted that he could not relax—too bad. Coffey at golf. He didn't care. Every existence its own rules. A long drive ahead on the rough, dusty road. He didn't mind that.

He had one vice which he could not explain or put a word to, which made him sick to bring to mind. It intruded in his dreams. But he was still a young man, although considered old for his years, and he could and would expunge it.

He had a flat at Fitzroy Falls and skinned his knuckle changing the wheel. He almost wept with the feeling of being so jangled, so rattled. It was the body turning on itself.

Back on the dusty road down the mountain.

A question kept coming to him. Who had, in all hell, made the telephone trunk call to the city. A trunk-line call.

Whoever made the call had something in them. But it was still unforgivable—the bringing-in of outside people to handle town problems.

That old buzzard Simon would never have talked on a telephone in his life, but he had a feeling it was him.

For George, the weekend had pulled apart like a bad soldering job.

Thelma expressed surprise at his early return and asked if he'd had a "nice time".

He said business was no picnic.

He went to the bathroom, locked himself in to bathe his jarred thumb and skinned knuckles.

Clarifying Muddy Water

•

The water-supply from the local river was so muddy at times that it would not go through a filter. George found that to overcome this problem he agitated each barrel of water with two pounds of phosphate of lime and then allowed it to settle. Most of the impurities went to the bottom of the barrel within minutes. The water could then be filtered.

One Drink That Did not "Catch On"

•

During the twenties George, in partnership with a local poultry farmer, tried to introduce a number of egg drinks. This is one, which together with the others, did not gain public acceptance.

HOT EGG LEMONADE

One egg, juice of one lemon, 3 tablespoons of powdered sugar. Beat the egg with the lemon juice and sugar thoroughly. Mix while adding the hot water. Serve with grated nutmeg and cinnamon. The amount of lemon juice and sugar may be varied to taste. Serve hot.

THE END OF ICE

WE are but the engine-drivers of progress," T. George McDowell said, moving a paperweight as if by calculation, as if it were a driving-lever, a switch, a throttle.

"Is friendship superseded?"

"Ice and candles, Jim, ice and candles—" balancing the two words—"ice-making belongs with candles—and the one-horse shay, and red-flannel underwear."

Jim Tutman without spirit said that electric refrigeration in the homes would break down—people would die in their sleep from escaping gas. They would come back to the safety of ice. And, anyhow, many homes would not be able to afford electricity, ever.

"No, Jim."

The unpleasant paradox for T. George was that he felt a love for ice. He had a great personal need for ice. He became unsettled when he was somewhere farther down the coast where ice was not available. He liked an ice-chilled soft drink. God bless the carbonated drink. Not only did he make 'em: he loved 'em. And sometimes on a hot day he would hold an ice-chip in his palm and look deep into the ice, into the slivers of trapped oxygen, and philosophize.

Staring into the ice, he could not help but believe that there was another silent, possible world inside the ice. He was not talking divinity. He would not recognize a god if he saw one coming down the main street in an automobile. But ice did not destroy. It preserved. Nothing disintegrated, nothing decayed in ice. Therefore it was related to life: not death. There could, for instance, be a civilization frozen under the North or South Poles. Bodies and cities frozen in ice. He thought maybe one day they would in fact freeze those who died. Awaiting the scientific means of restoring life. Whom to restore? With all due respect to the sanctity of life there were some people he would not wish to restore. He proposed those who had achieved success in their own lifetime.

James Tutman was a borderline case.

Jim should have changed over to the household electrical refrigerator business instead of doggedly going on making ice.

Jim had made only a half-success of life. He had pioneered the ice business in this town, home delivery, ice-chests. But all that was finished.

It was not that men hate progress: but that they love inertia.

Man's know-how was his personal capital. The bank inside the head. It was once said that it was wise to invest in knowledge because no man could steal it from you. No longer true.

It was the closing of the bank doors for Jim. What he had learned in life was no longer valid currency.

A man was nothing more than what he knew and what he could do. He had no time for people without vocation. Not that Tutman was one of these. He had vocation—was passionately, or had been, devoted to a craft. But Jim's vocation was disappearing from the face of the earth.

Jim Tutman, "refrigeration engineer", one-time chairman of the Chamber of Commerce, Rotarian, had once had the Premier of the State stay overnight in his home, had entertained Inventors and Aviators, and was, in fact, an Inventor himself, in small ways. Some in the town swore that Tutman had invented the block of ice. But this, of course, was not the case. Now here was Jim in his office, frowning, uncomfortable, had put on a tie, to seek a sustaining loan from him, T. George McDowell, a man his junior.

T. George found this sad. That it was a compliment to his own acumen, he appreciated only in passing.

T. George looked at Jim Tutman—at the sinews, warts, hairs, skin, bristles, freckles, pores, a face that had looked at and solved many problems—and as if by x-ray saw the white-bone skull with eyeless sockets.

His hand perspired on the paperweight.

Thought of the death-white skull made him queasy.

"I shouldn't have to tell *you* this, Jim, but I will," he said conclusively. "It's time to modernize the mind. To modernize the mind."

There was silence.

Then Tutman offensively, T. George felt, disregarded this

advice and said, "You're letting me go to bankruptcy?"

T. George said nothing.

"God in heaven, George, I helped you get your start in this town." Tutman stopped, having problems with words. Tutman was no speechmaker. Speechmaking, thought George, was the total person talking. Hands, face, mouth, body. Not like the letter or the telephone. Learn the first and last sentence—then you'll begin well and end well.

Tutman seemed to give up. The total person was talking all right. In Tutman's every movement. Tutman said with bitterness, "You and your damned Rotary guff about the Brotherhood of Business."

"I repaid, Jim."

Tutman rose. The tension of his clutch had curled and creased the brim of his hat which he'd held in his hand throughout the talk. Tutman's face was set with frustration. The photograph on the wall caught his eye and he pushed his chair away, going across to it, now jerking with anger, nodding with anger at it.

It was a photograph of them both, smiling together, glasses held in toast, back in the twenties, at the installation of the Bratby syruping, filling and crowning machine. Tutman had helped. The rosy days of friendship and the allegiance of equals.

Tutman tore the picture from its hook and, throwing it to the floor, stomped on it with his boot, shattering the glass, and probably, T. George couldn't see, probably tearing the photograph.

All motion causes friction.

It all existed there in the broken glass and silence after Tutman left. T. George felt his thighs and backside moist on the chair. He stood up pulling his sweaty trousers from his legs. A book, *Increase Your Powers of Concentration,* manifested itself from the other objects in the office and then dissolved back into the total whole. The detail and the whole. T. George became aware of them then. He had not philosophized about the detail and the whole. We know, he thought, that the whole contains infinite detail, detail beyond observation. We at times had to see the whole and not be led to the infinite detail where a man could lose himself for life. If detail manifested itself, it was to tell you something—something which would illuminate the whole.

Yes.

Now the broken photograph was gone and he saw only the still, total room—a blur of detail. Pull the switch—now only the broken photograph existed in his vision and the room was gone. Some men were detail workers who never saw a vision. Some men were visionaries who never got the job done.

A Secret of Life: to conceive the vision: to pursue the vision: yet have the patience to supervise the detail.

The Life Purpose of a business man is to get the produce of genius to the market-place for ordinary people.

Move with the Times or be moved over by the Times.

The job of the salesman is to convince people to improve their lives.

The policeman's widow. The policeman's widow at the show dance had danced the tango with him and he had found his body excited by her to the point of embarrassment. She had known this and had purposely leaned against him, time and time again. Had rolled her stomach and thigh against his groin. Tantalizing him. After one unfaithful occasion, shortly after, he had resolved never again to acknowledge her. His judgement subdued the roaring protest of his body. He never again acknowledged her, despite, at first, her puzzled, hurt smiles in the street. Her notes, calls, and entreaties.

The only person he mentioned it to was Tutman, who told him to go ahead and enjoy himself. "It might soften you up, George."

He disregarded this advice.

The flesh, the passions have no special rights or claims on the behaviour.

Take the leverless fountain pen. The leverless fountain pen is an applaudable work of genius, but he had no doubts that it would be superseded. This was not because he could see anything wrong with the leverless fountain pen, or because he knew what would replace it. He knew it would be replaced because he believed in the implacable laws of progress. Perhaps an electrical pen which transmitted words the way the telephone transmitted voice? He put that only as a suggestion.

To move with Progress one had to shake free of the clutching, bony hand of the past. Men always thought in terms of the past. Take himself. He had thought of an electrical "pen". Why pen? Simply because the pen preceded. Look at refrigeration. At first thousands of pounds were spent trying to make a refrigerator which would freeze a block of ice in the top. Imitating the ice-chest. But the answer had been absorption refrigeration. Extracting the heat to make cold. Inventive men knew how to give the past the slip.

When and why did a man lose the faculty of change? Was it some point in the dying of the mind and body. A hardening of the nervous system. He practised keeping his mind agile. Daily he made himself think thoughts he had not thought before. He forced himself to consider the worst. He practised considering the opposite. He tried always to imagine at least two other possible ways of doing something. He fed his mind with maxims and precepts—the how-to-do-it manual of the mind.

The shattered photograph of those earlier, united days. Motion caused friction. It was the deepest mystery of life that this should be so. That change always hurt someone. Why the human race had to pay for its advancement. There were always rats in the cellar of life. It was a fact of mechanical life that without friction we could have perpetual motion.

He picked up the fragments of glass. F-dash it. He picked up the damaged framed photograph and put it away in the bottom drawer of the desk. F-dash.

Jim Tutman had been an experimenter, when he was a boy. He had shared the experiments with Tutman, transfixed with awe and anxiety.

In those happier childhood days.

Tutman had a "laboratory". In a shed at the back of the house down the paddock. Stoppered bottles of chemicals. Liquids and powders of dangerous colours, blue-edged labels, the riveting words POISON and EXPLOSIVE. The invisible, floating presence of sulphur, ammonia, chlorine, and various oxides which pinched at the nostrils. Electrical batteries.

Tutman had cylinders of gas. He had a 2 h.p. American kerosene engine. Tutman's father indulged him. Considered him a genius. He also, in those days, considered Tutman a genius. Tutman's father probably didn't know at first, looking back, just how elaborate and how dangerous the set-up in the shed had been.

Tutman played around with the early refrigerants. He was always making ice with maniacal ecstasy.

He would ride his horse into town on Sunday afternoons and go straight to Tutman's laboratory.

"Want to see me freeze a mouse?"

A white mouse would be taken from Tutman's breeding cage.

He would choke back pity and watch the white mouse, pink-nosed, freeze in a jar in a flurry of squeaks and twistings.

The ice would form and finally in the clear, solid ice, as if in a glass case, the mouse would be held, paw and nose against the ice.

He'd always been disappointed, always hoping that when the ice melted the mouse would still be alive. The mouse never revived. They experimented with resuscitation, using electrical shocks, but they never succeeded.

There was an explosive device, or so Tutman said, and traps of other kinds for anyone who tried to break into the shed. Tutman talked of a "secret ray". Tutman hinted that he would be pleased to see someone try to break into the laboratory—to test the effectiveness of the traps.

"Want to see some fireworks?"

He had seen Tutman's gunpowder and home-made fireworks many times.

Tutman lost a finger that way.

The doctor had been unable to find the finger. Tutman had, in fact, put it in his pocket.

Tutman showed him the finger later in a jar of formalin. Tutman preserved the tattered finger for amusement.

To have given money to Tutman now, these many years later, would have been to risk catching one's own hand in the Cogs of Progress. Tutman, who had always been so ahead of his times, had fallen behind and was lost.

Hallstrom, the Kelvinator, the Leonard refrigerator, and the Cogs of Progress were destroying him. He could always find work—at the dairy factory, maybe.

But he realized that Tutman would never work for wages. He was the independent business man, inventor. In recent years, brooding, drinking, allowing himself and his business to run down.

Why, he'd suggested to Tutman time and time again that the system of ice delivery to the home was the weak point in his organization.

Ice-men dripping water through the house, the unshaven ice-men with their hessian bags. No good. Not modern. They were always hired for their muscle, never for their appearance. They should have been Ambassadors of Ice. And the size of the blocks shrinking in the sun.

He had suggested to Tutman an ice servery. A flap in the wall of the house so that the ice could be put through into the ice-chest from the outside. Night deliveries. But Tutman stopped thinking somewhere in the late twenties. Shut down his mind. He had at one time suggested to Tutman a partnership in his own cordial-making business, maybe going into ice-cream. That was some years back. Thank god, Tutman had not taken up the offer.

It did no good to fist-fight with refrigerator salesmen in the street. Or to heckle Hallstrom at the Show demonstrations.

We are but the engine-drivers of Progress—we do not make the timetable.

He learned by telephone message next day that James Tutman had disappeared during the night, leaving his wife, his two almost grown children, and a bankrupt ice-making business.

He was, as a man of feeling, disturbed by the news. It was quite a knock. But as a realist he was somewhat relieved. Supposing of course that he had simply left town. Gone to some other town.

He did not admire himself for his sense of relief, but, on the other hand, did not relish facing Tutman in the street or seeing him decline into god-knows-what. Somehow it was best, he felt in the hours following the news, that Tutman rule off the book at this point. The town could care for his wife.

Tutman was a lesson. He himself was considering going into shop and café refrigeration. Keeping up. The domestic refrigerator could well mean the end of wholesale ice-cream, and he had decided against that idea. With electric refrigeration people would be making ice-cream in their homes.

Tutman was a lesson for us all.

Tutman's sunburned body was found some days later in the bush not far from town. The post-mortem showed that it had been death by cyanide poisoning, which caused much comment and reached the city papers. His wife testified that for a year or so Tutman had carried in his pocket a small phial of cyanide. She had beseeched him not to be morbid. He had even prepared a phial for her and the children. She described her husband as in a state of chronic depression. He said the town had turned its back on him. No longer needed him. His career had come to an end before his life had run its course.

The local paper incorrectly stated that Tutman had invented the block of ice.

How Tutman Froze the Mouse

•

George thought that Tutman froze the mouse by first preparing
a ten per cent dilution of sulphuric acid in water. He chilled this
and then placed it in a stone jug. He added a handful of Glauber's
salts for each quart of solution. The mouse, in a tube of water,
was immersed in the solution, which dropped dramatically
in temperature.

Why Ice Is Superior to a Refrigerator

●

1. Ice is instantly ready for use and begins to cool the food immediately.
2. Ice carries humidity and moisture necessary for food preservation. There is no dehydration of the food.
3. Refrigerators create "dry cold", which takes the moisture from the food.
4. Gas could leak from a refrigerator, causing sickness or even death.
5. Ice is a natural product, existing in nature.
6. Ice keeps a uniform temperature and does not vary with the electrical current.
7. Ice-cooling is silent.

Measuring the Weight of Ice

•

This is a method which may serve to remove unjust suspicions or to detect short weight. Multiply the length, breadth and thickness of a block of ice in inches and divide by thirty. This will give, very closely, the weight in pounds.

RULES AND PRACTICES FOR THE OVERCOMING OF SHYNESS

RULES AND PRACTICES FOR THE OVERCOMING OF SHYNESS

1. Always walk up to a man as if he owes you money.
2. Train yourself to look at the bridge of the other man's nose, to give the impression that you are staring him straight in the eye.
3. Speak out with a loud voice and you will finish strongly: begin weakly and you will finish weakly.
4. Sometimes to be heard amid the shouting it is necessary to speak softly.
5. Learn when to remain silent, thus forcing the other fellow to speak.
6. Before meeting with a stranger, make a list of conversational items.
7. Learn the beginning and the end of a speech, so that you begin and end fluently.
8. Go out of your way to meet the Great. Keep the company of those older and superior to yourself. By doing so, you will gain knowledge and, at the same time, gain confidence through observing the weaknesses and foibles of your superiors.
9. Joust with your shyness by putting it constantly to the test.
10. Remember that these are but tricks and rules. Learn your trade well. Self-confidence grows from ability, as does your value as a person in the society of men.

Even so, in 1936, George McDowell was still dogged by shyness. The typed-out rules hung, pasted on cardboard, but he had to admit they'd become somewhat a fixture in the office. But also, he sincerely hoped, a fixture in his mind.

His experience with American Rotary during a visit to that country as a young man had convinced him of the need to overcome the unconfident reserve in the Australian character and the shyness so painfully hobbling his own character. Yet one had to avoid also the adolescent boisterousness and Sentimental Bloke cockiness which the working-class used to conceal their inferiority. In a talk only recently to his own Rotary Club he had recalled that visit and said, "We need to cultivate bonhomie and, to some extent, 'abandon' (there had been some winking, a rustle of chuckles at this). As business men we come to dinner bearing the impression of the day's work, but we need to throw this aside as far as is humanly possible and give ourselves up more to a free exhibition of fellowship."

The words expressed his own deep yearning and in some ways his deepest regret that at thirty-three he was known as a man difficult at times to approach and of formal manner.

Although this appealed to him as an image also of "strong character", he did try at times to relax it. He diligently learned jokes to tell so as to put people at ease, especially staff and such, but, no, he was a stiff man. He didn't drink, which was a drawback.

He'd even been embarrassed when, after giving his talk, "Bonhomie—the French Have a Word for It", he was approached by a visiting Rotarian from Nowra who congratulated him on the talk and asked for concrete suggestions on how to achieve this "bonhomie".

He could only repeat in a rather unhelpful way the idea of "stunts" at club meetings, which was an American idea.

What he thought, but could not get out with any clarity, was that "making a fool" of oneself, or at least "playing the fool", was a way of "getting outside oneself".

Yet one had to know how to play the fool without becoming a fool. And he opposed alcohol at club meetings on the grounds of standards. Meetings could become nothing more than smokos with blue jokes, which was not what Rotary was about nor what he had in mind. No, he wanted a sort of circumscribed and clean playing-up, but he had not made it at all clear and nothing came of his talk. He heard later that after he'd left, a few of the jokers at the club had chosen to take his talk the wrong way and to suggest that he had some pretty wild schemes for livening up the meetings. There was always someone who never missed an opportunity to take things the wrong way. Sometimes, he thought, joking was used to chase away an idea.

His life was a Shyness Test.

He was shy but not *timid*. He drove his spirit into combat with shyness, and although on each occasion he defeated shyness, it came back, shyness returned, refreshed.

He went out of his way to meet the great. He'd met Paul Harris, founder of Rotary, on his recent visit to Australia. He'd met the American writer, Zane Grey, down at Bermagui. But this year one event, more than all others in his life, had seemed to diminish his shyness, terrorize it even, so that it receded as a factor in his life.

The event was his burning-down of the Crowhurst house.

H. C. Crowhurst, retired accountant, old friend of George's father, had lived with his two aged sisters, who both predeceased him eighteen and twenty months respectively, and his will stated that, there being no surviving relatives, their house and its contents were to be destroyed by fire.

"I do not wish strangers to trespass on, or have the use of, that which my dear sisters and I cherished, shared, and partook of, throughout our lifetimes together on this earth." The will named George as executor.

Crowhurst had declined in the last year, rarely coming down to the town, although he had, until a few years back, done George's books. George out of respect for his father's old friends had continued the weekly call, expecting as he walked up the path, on each visit to the house on the hill among the Norfolk pines, to find old Harry dead.

As it happened, the District Nurse had been the one to find old Harry dead.

George had at first made some remarks, along with the rest, about the seemingly wanton destruction but inwardly found the commission emotionally quickening, lured by its abnormality. Such an unnatural act for the town, striving as it was to shape itself, the homes and shops along the gravel streets, to make itself a normal town along with the rest in the State. But just this once he was quickened, and allowed himself to be. He went along with the unnatural act which had befallen him. He kept, however, a solemn face when confirming the legality of the will with Sime, a city lawyer.

For weeks he gave detailed and private consideration to the technique for burning the house and its contents. He even thought of explosives. He tried to talk confidentially and scientifically about it with Tutman, a scientifically minded friend from childhood. Tutman in the old days would have entered into it with relish but now lacked the spark. Tutman had sunk personally through business and other difficulties, maintaining a false sense of superiority by mixing now with inferiors in the public bars.

So he ended up doing it alone and was glad.

Although he told only the local fire brigade and police sergeant, the word got around, and children and others drifted up to the house on the hill to see it burn.

He began by drenching the contents of the house with kerosene. One musty room after another. Sloshing the kerosene over the lace doilies, the crocheted tableclothes, the antimacassars, the rotted brown flowers in vases, the worn arm chairs, where Crowhurst and the sisters had sat each evening for fifty years or more, the potted ferns, the bamboo hall stands. The books of Keats, Kipling, and the complete novels of Sir Walter Scott. The oilskin on the kitchen table, the kitchen smelling of toast, preserves, lysol, and carbolic.

He drenched the concertina files of letters, the spiked receipts, dockets, years of petty transaction.

Backhouse, from the local newspaper, joined him and wanted to remove the books.

"A crime, George. Give them to the School of Arts."

He respected reading and agreed with Backhouse about the crime, thinking as he did that he had never committed a crime, and thinking then that this was not legally a crime, yet resembled criminality. However, he told Backhouse, one undertook a commission in every detail and to the detail, or not at all. "I'm that sort of person."

"I know you're that sort of person, George."

He went on drenching. Backhouse shook his head.

Backhouse's disapproval and the books in the bookcase soon to be aflame opened a throttle in him and he vibrated inwardly with the complete unnaturalness of it, the permitted unnaturalness of it. He drenched the rows of books with great vigour, seeing the kerosene spread and seek its way down the spines, running along the gutters of dust at the tops of the books. Literary genius about to burn. His spirit, far from quailing, was empowered.

Paintings hung on the wall—of English villages and rustic scenes—none, he'd been told, of high value. He drenched those too.

The Hoe Man. He stopped at the painting of the Hoe Man and remembered Hubbard's lines: "Let us all hoe a little and then the hoe man will not for ever be looking at the soil."

"What is it, George?" Backhouse's voice reached him distantly. "Second thoughts?"

"I was thinking of the Hoe Man."

"You know the poem?" Backhouse seemed surprised.

"No—an essay by Elbert Hubbard."

Backhouse smiled, knowingly. "I didn't think it would be the poem."

"I maybe read the poem, but I don't recall its wording."

"Not actually your sort of sentiments, George."

He didn't ask Backhouse what he meant.

He went on with the drenching, soaking the carpets. He found his breathing came out with irregularity because of excitation, but he made out, in front of Backhouse, that it was from exertion.

He wished damned Backhouse, with his enigmatic remarks, would go away.

"It's a damn' pity in a way," he said, covering his feelings, to appease Backhouse, to get him on side.

"You seem to be enjoying it, George."

Backhouse was a strange fish.

Intelligent enough, but one was never really sure that he was *agreeing* or just listening for his own private meanings. He asked more questions than he ever printed in his paper. What did he do with all the information he got? Where did it go? He never let on whether you had convinced him. He never voted on anything.

He then said to Backhouse, without reserve, because of the irritating presence of Backhouse, and because he felt strong from having the commission, "God, you're right. Yes, I am enjoying it. Yes."

And went on with the drenching. That, oddly enough, seemed to please Backhouse. The admission of the enjoyment.

"Watch out, George—I'm not part of the contents—I'm not to be burnt." Some kerosene splashed onto Backhouse's shoes.

The house had not been connected to the town electricity. Crowhurst always said he liked the "soft" light of gas and the lantern, and that electricity gave "hard" light. No amount of talking could change his mind.

He drenched the three single beds in the three separate rooms.

The women's clothing in the wardrobes, some dating from the turn of the century, hanging there since the death of the sisters.

"That's enough, George—they're hellishly old. They'll burn well enough."

George ignored Backhouse and threw some more kerosene over the women's clothing.

He emptied the drum and went outside to the Chev to get the third drum. He did the inside walls, the wallpaper coming clean as the kerosene carried away the dust.

Then he and the police sergeant—Backhouse declining to assist—lugged in bales of straw and placed one or two in each room against the walls, drenching them also with kerosene.

Outside he saw some shaking of heads.

George knew of the bad feeling about the burning. A deputation from the local Labor League and a union official from the city had tried to get an injunction. Talk about giving the house to an unemployed family.

No one appreciated the effect of the Depression and its causes more than George. He had organized a debate on the matter in town quite early. He had used the word Depression when it became necessary. He'd set the Spend for Employment Scheme rolling at Rotary. He'd built a warehouse when his judgement told him to wait a year. It had however turned out well except that he could not get the staff and others to call it "the warehouse". They all called it the shed.

As for the house and the will. George was governed, he felt, by this view: I have been given a commission: I have to carry it through to execution against all obstacles: others may feel it their duty to create obstacles: my duty is to overcome these: I am irrevocably deputed.

I am irrevocably deputed.

He told the Labor League that when one carried out a commission, one could not consider and weigh the complete chain of implication, the full stretch of possibilities. People who did achieved nothing, intimidated by the unforeseen. Frozen in their tracks. All activity, he told them, had consequences which could not be foreseen. Tradition, law and experience guarded against consequences which could be foreseen. One had to know, within tradition and law, when to stop consideration, have the courage to proceed into unforeseen consequences—in a word, to get on with the job.

They had not been convinced.

There'd been a story about town, too, that the house contained money, which would be burnt. There was no money. And he would not burn money.

The fire brigade, out of breath, and in pieces of uniform, pulled their reel up the hill to the house. The water pressure, anyhow, too low, as it always was at the end of summer.

They couldn't have done much if the house did get out of control. Still, they stationed themselves about the grounds with beaters.

Crowhurst had been a stamp collector through his life, and had specifically stated that the collection too was to be burnt. It was considered, in conversation about the town, to be the most valuable thing in the house. He and Backhouse leafed through the thousands of stamps, right up to date with a complete set of the new German stamps.

George placed no value on stamp-collecting—misspent time. You could not eat it nor hang it on a wall.

He told Backhouse his thoughts about it, and Backhouse

seemed to give the opinion some credit.

To the detail. As the last act he sloshed the kerosene over the stamp albums, opened to allow easier burning. Opened at random pages, the kerosene running over the impassive faces of monarchs, dictators, emperors, triangular stamps, brightly coloured from islands of the South Seas.

The face of aviators, generals, and explorers.

The twenty or so albums lay on a bench, the meticulously fixed stamps glued there by Crowhurst the schoolboy and then Crowhurst the old man, representing the power and the glory of all the nation states.

Backhouse left at this point, saying that he didn't want to watch any more.

George finished the drenching and came out for fresh air, away from the kerosene fumes, wiping his brow with his sleeve. The small crowd were talking with the firemen, children playing with the useless fire-hose reel.

He went to the sergeant. "About ready, Herbert," he said seriously. "Hot work."

They smiled at the unintended joke.

He spoke to the captain of the brigade, who got the men back to their places with their beaters.

He opened all the windows for draught.

He was rather pleased with the crowd, although it had been intended that there should be no spectators.

He went to the car and got out the blow-torch, which he had decided would be the most suitable method of lighting the house.

He put on his coat.

He'd given it some thought. It was, after all, an official act.

He lit the blow-torch and pumped it until it roared.

He looked across at the firemen and the sergeant and nodded. They nodded back.

The crowd stopped talking.

He pulled out a piece of paper from his side coat-pocket and read, "I, George McDowell, executor of this estate, hereby consign this house and all its contents to ashes in accordance with the wishes of the late Herbert Charles

Crowhurst as expressed in his last will and testament."

The blow-torch roaring.

Backhouse, he noticed, had not gone but was standing one foot on the running-board of his car, in a pose of dissociation.

George moved into the house, the roaring torch in his hand, touching the bales of straw and other well-soaked places with the blue flame of the torch. He stopped at the stamp albums and held the torch to them, burning a black hole straight through the faces of the monarchs, dictators, emperors, page after page curled away into ash.

Through the bedrooms and the women's clothing. The house filled quickly with crackling and smoke.

He realized he was lingering in the house. The house, dry from summer, was igniting around him. The paintings on the walls were aflame. The dining-room table was alight, the fruit bowl burning.

He was lingering. Run. He almost had to instruct himself to run.

He was held there in the igniting house, as if testing his invulnerability.

Run. He instructed himself again.

He came out the front door, eyes watering, and pulled himself stiffly together. Brushed ash from his clothing.

The firemen had stationed themselves too close and now moved back. The crowd oo-ahed as the flames came fingering out the windows, and they too moved back. George decided to move his car. So did Backhouse.

Woomph, perhaps a lantern exploding.

The house roof shingles began to fall in.

In all, the house and contents took two and a quarter hours to burn to the ground. All that remained was a blackened cement washtub, a bath with four squat legs. A Bega stove and the chimney.

The intention was that the rubble would be carted away and the land was then to be auctioned, with the proceeds going to Lodge Abercorn, of which Crowhurst had been a member.

No trace would be left of the Crowhurst family, which had

lived in the town almost since it was incorporated as a municipality.

Later, George could not remember when his body had been more alive, the conflagration raced through him as through the house. It left him burned out, tired, and he went to sleep for a few hours, something he had never done before—sleep during the day. Never.

He felt it somehow indecent to talk about it now that it was over and done, but he did say to Thelma that very few men in a lifetime had the opportunity to burn the home and possessions of another human.

He considered it had helped to burn away his shyness, although it was a rule and practice which one could not put on the list. The burning of the house, together with his meeting with Paul Harris, founder of Rotary, made 1936 a memorable year and one of both public and personal progress, although, Thelma said, some people thought he'd become hard and unyielding because of the burning.

The Man with the Hoe

•

The confusion between Backhouse and George about the
painting comes about because there are three things titled
"The Man with the Hoe"—a painting, a poem, and an essay.
First, the painting by Millet, which George was admiring
before burning. The poem referred to by Backhouse was by
Edwin Markham and was inspired by Millet's painting.
It goes in part:

> Bowed by the weight of centuries he leans
> Upon his hoe and gazes on the ground,
> The emptiness of ages on his face,
> And on his back the burden of the world.
> Who made him dead to rapture and despair,
> A thing that grieves not and that never hopes,
> Stolid and stunned, a brother to the ox?
> Who loosened and let down this brutal jaw?
> Whose was the hand that slanted back this brow?
> Whose breath blew out the light within the brain?

It goes on to deal with the exploitation of the labouring class and ends:

> *O masters, lords and rulers in all lands,*
> *How will the future reckon with this Man?*
> *How answer his brute question in that hour,*
> *When whirlwinds and rebellion shake the world?*
> *How will it be within Kingdoms and with Kings*
> *With those who shaped him to the thing he is,*
> *When this dumb terror shall reply to God*
> *After the silence of centuries?*

Ambrose Bierce said at the time that the poem had all the life of a dead fish.

George had only read the essay by Elbert Hubbard inspired by the poem. He had not read the original poem nor, until that day, seen the painting which inspired the poem.

GEORGE McDOWELL DELIVERS A MESSAGE TO GENERAL JUAN GARCIA OF THE CUBAN ARMY

❧

I N 1924, after a visit to the United States with his father, George McDowell returned to the town to begin his life. He returned with three passions, he thought—Rotary— the aerated drinks business—and the possibilities of town electricity.

About Rotary he could do very little. It had not come to the South Coast and he lacked the standing and age to do much about it. But the manufacture of aerated soft drinks, with the help of a loan from a business man friend, became his vocation. Although Australia did not have prohibition, which had helped the American industry, he believed ice-chests and refrigeration would allow people to chill drinks in their homes and encourage them to buy bottled drinks.

Nor could he forward the possibilities of electricity until the town had a generator, and he consequently became vocal about this. He joined the Science Club regardless of its reputation as a hotbed of atheism. His business man friend, James Tutman, local inventor and ice maker, had nominated him. In the Science Club he could at least talk and speculate on electricity and experiment on Demonstration Night with devices, although he was, himself, no inventor. He said that he was simply a person who could move an idea from point A to point B without damaging it (sometimes improving it) and without losing it in transit. Which always got a good laugh and was a modest-enough thing to say.

He knew in his private mind that he was ahead of his times. Even ahead of Tutman on many things. Tutman knew more about ice, but when you came to look at him, he knew very little else. He was ahead of Tutman philosophically. He sometimes thought that, in truth, he was something of a "visionary".

But, be that as it may, he was anyhow the youngest independent business man in town. He was commonly described as "a live wire".

One weekend he and Doctor Trenbow took their blanket roll and groundsheet to walk to the bottomless pit and, on behalf of the Science Club, to measure the depth of the so-called bottomless pit.

As they picked and slid their way through the sandstone bush, he told the doctor that he would be putting a grape juice in the shops next summer.

"I drink them myself for three weeks," he said, "as a test." Hoping that would satisfy the doctor about purity.

They clambered down a gully, sliding now and then on their heels, sending one or two rocks bouncing down. George talked about the possibility of ice-cream wholesaling. "Say the word 'wholesale' and people think 'city'. Need not be. A country town could wholesale to the city. Why take our milk more than a hundred miles to buy it back as city ice-cream. As it is now each shop has its own recipe and some don't have the first idea. Can't get it cold enough for a start. Some of it's no more than custard. I'll take the best recipe, or the best two or three. Try them all. I'll put it out as the town ice-cream. Take soft drinks. In the United States Dr Pepper is sold thousands of miles from where it's made. Take flavoured milk. No one has really done much with flavoured milk. First you need go-ahead cafés which put in refrigeration. The South Coast could do it. Our shopkeepers go with the times. First you need reliable electricity."

George panting, realized, as they pushed through the snagging bush, that he was gabbling again and pulled himself up, changed to a more reserved demeanour.

"You're alive with ambition, George," the doctor said.

The doctor said it in a way that meant he himself was not.

"As a doctor you're a member of a very learned profession", in case the doctor felt inadequate.

"All a matter of meeting requirements, George. Now you—you're headed for the uncharted territory."

Yes, by golly, thought George, new products are like that.

The space between conversation was becoming longer as their energy leaked away into the bush, as the bush dragged at their attention, and the bush dullness settled on them.

"Influenced by America, George?" the doctor asked at a stop.

"Rotary could be bigger than governments."

"You think so?"

Little more was said between them until camp.

By the time they made camp, they had what the doctor called "bush stumbles" from the scrub, foothold finding, wading through knee-high fern, rock clambering. George also suffered from the overbearing darkness of the bush as they went farther from the township. He kept seeing in his mind the scattered smoky houses, the long green grass of the unbuilt-on blocks, the shops which still didn't link to make a solid row, his factory, and the two saw mills nibbling away at the huge endless bush surrounding the town, turning it into building planks. Always in the bush he realized impatiently how little a hold they had yet on the coast. The thin white line of dusty habitation between the sea and the unsettled mountains. He urgently wanted for the land to be cleared and the roads properly made.

They both dozed for an hour or so and then, clumsy with fatigue, made the fire. As they sat there gazing, doped, at the camp fire, they let out with pieces of conversation, like broken biscuits. Tired talk. George went on a little about his ideas for beach kiosks when the rail came down the coast.

The doctor listened, sipping his rum while George sipped his tea.

The doctor made a surprise shift in the conversation.

"What about divinity, George?" the doctor asked, after which they sat without talking in the croaking night.

The doctor was a known sceptic.

George thought about what he could say judiciously, considering the town, and how to please the doctor, and then about what he really believed, and found that the wide night sky, the mesmerizing camp fire, the blackness of the bush, compelled him to try to assemble his true ideas.

The doctor got up before George answered, and urinated, too close to the camp fire for George's way of thinking. The doctor always washed his hands before instead of after, because he said his hands were dirtier than his privates.

"I suppose," he began when the doctor was back, "that I don't believe in God—I mean a god with shape or residence."

That seemed a good start. Sometimes the words were there

in the mouth and sometimes not.

"But goodwill—that's a sort of divinity, the sort I would believe. I try to tread the footpath of goodwill."

George looked at the doctor and then at the coals, having not found a reaction in the doctor's face. He then said something about people needing divinity when they had nothing else, no faith in themselves. But not for those who could look after themselves.

"Haven't you worried about your purpose in creation—about man's place in nature? Are we, for instance, Lords of Nature?" The doctor waved his hand at the bush darkness, the starry sky. "Do the trees hear us?"

George had never thought whether the trees could hear. He heard the questions and felt a long way from them, they did not belong in his mind. No, he had not and did not consider such things.

"Or," the doctor went on, "the great questions of Civics—how to control those with power, why some are rich and some are poor, why some men the masters?"

George was conscious that the doctor was a university-educated man. He himself had never considered going to university. He had always wanted to become a business man. But he held the highest respect, all the same, for men with degrees.

He pulled his mind back to the doctor's big questions. He tried again to say how he thought. "No, I don't ask. I live by the rules inherent in the job at hand. Every trade has its own rules inherent in it."

But he was not a tradesman.

"Every Science too, and every Craft—even, say, the Science of aerated drinks has its rules inherent. I suppose I believe that when you follow the rules of the craft, the big questions look after themselves. That when you arrive at the Big Questions, if you've followed the rules inherent in your craft, the answers will be obvious."

Yes, that was what he thought. Yes.

"I'm not sure I follow," the doctor said with interest.

George said that, in manufacturing and employing labour

and engaging in commerce, you found natural rules which supplied the answers and suggested what position had to be taken.

"I'm against governments interfering with working arrangements between people. Unions too. Unions are the idea of city men who want power. Unions produce nothing."

"That's quite a philosophy, George."

George looked at the doctor to see if he was being mocked. He did not feel that it was quite a "philosophy"—they were his opinions. Mostly expressed for the first time.

"While the theorists and the theologians worry, men like you make the system work. Even if it doesn't work well."

The doctor drank more rum.

"Yes," the doctor said, "you justify your life each day— to a customer."

Again, as far as George could tell, it was without mockery, yet without flattery. And again, the doctor talked as if he was not one of those who made the world run yet maybe not a philosopher either.

George tried again to say something important, to reach a point where he felt he had said sufficient, made his stand, he wanted to have said *enough*. He felt he had said nothing.

"I make things people want," he added.

The doctor, maybe, nodded.

"Where there is a conflict between the new and the old, I'd always be with the new," George went on, trying to find a list of his beliefs.

"Until you yourself grow old, George." The doctor smiled across at him.

In the camp-fire light George flushed, realizing he'd said an immature thing. It stung. Everyone said he was older than his years. For instance, here he was talking philosophy with the doctor. But most of all George did not want to show his youth, or to make slips.

The maddening thing was that he *was* a philosopher. Damn it. How to get this across because he didn't philosophize about the things the doctor postulated.

"And what about the good life, George?"

"What? How do you mean?"

"The good life—wine, food, women and song."

"I don't have much time," George mumbled, blushing for his inexperience in these areas. "What with getting started in life." He put wood on the fire.

"And what books, George, what books have influenced you?"

George thought. He considered himself a Reader. But now he found he couldn't recollect any books. Manuals about cordials and their manufacture. Herbert Casson's business library. An I.C.S. course. Things like that. But they were not what the doctor meant.

"*The Message to Garcia*," he said, remembering. Of course.

"*The Message to Garcia*," the doctor repeated, with a tone George could not interpret.

"I was given a specially printed copy when in America—by Edward J. Nowak, of St Louis, a cordial manufacturer there."

"How has it influenced you, George?"

Damn it. How *had* it influenced him?

"Well Rowan, he did the job. He got the job done. When asked by the President of the United States to take a message to General Garcia in the mountains of Cuba, Rowan didn't ask who Garcia was, how much he'd be paid, where he could find him, what was his address, whether to take a boat or a horse. He just said, 'Yes, sir', and took the message and went. He just took the message, and even though it took a long time against all obstacles, he delivered the message to Garcia. Rowan just did the job."

George stopped and thought, and then added, "It was initiative riding on tenacity."

The doctor didn't say anything.

"That's the highest personal development, isn't it, doctor?"

"What is, George?"

Hadn't he been listening? Or was it the rum?

"The difference between the Self-mover and those who need to be supervised and led."

"Maybe, George, but maybe we don't arrange things properly so that everyone can be a Self-mover."

The doctor didn't elaborate.

"No.—" on this George was firm—"no, there are those who are individual and energized and those who simply follow. Everywhere I look in life, and everything I see, confirms this."

They sat in silence then. The doctor still sipped rum.

George sipped tea.

"What if I asked you to go on a mission?" the doctor asked, breaking across the bush and fire noises.

"I'd go."

"Why?"

"You're the head of this . . . expedition."

Then George added, "To give orders, you have first to be able to take orders."

George saw that he would only take orders if it was a step towards giving them. So what.

The doctor smiled. George bridled. Well, it was true.

"What if I . . ." the doctor thought, "what if I asked you to find water . . . now . . . at this time of the night?" Waving at the black bush.

"I'd do it."

The conversation was adrift. Was moving to a whirlpool.

"Yes, I would go," George repeated, to the President of the United States.

"Even if it was just an 'exercise'."

George could see the distinction, but it didn't seem to operate against doing it. He could not see that it changed the imperative, the binding nature of an order.

"Yes."

The doctor stopped looking at the fire or the rum bottle and looked across at George.

"Well, do it," the doctor said, making a gesture with his mug of rum.

"Are you serious then?" George asked, firming his voice.

"Would what-his-name have asked that?"

"Andrew J. Rowan."

"Would Andrew J. Rowan have asked that question?"

Flushing, George without another word got up, took a billy, put on a sweater, and tiredly, stiffly, set off. He knew that water, if any, would be found at the bottom of the valley. Way, way down. There would be a creek of sorts at the bottom. Perhaps.

It took him well into the night to get to the bottom, after slipping, groping and being torn at by branches and undergrowth. After losing his footing, falling, grazing his hip, he found the stream by moonlight, scarcely trickling, but a stream, and there was water.

He said aloud in the wide, empty gorge, "General Garcia, I presume", without enjoying any humour.

Why!

Why, he did not really feel like Rowan at all and did not want to be Rowan. He wanted to be a Garcia.

I am a Garcia.

I am a Garcia, not a Rowan.

I am a general: not a messenger of this world.

He filled the billy, stood very still, looked all around at the stars and the black bush shapes, took a deep, cool breath, and started back.

The doctor was asleep when he stumbled back up with a billy of creek water, hardly any lost on the uphill climb.

George slept late into the morning despite the flies.

When he woke, the doctor had made tea and damper and also taken a reading of the depth of the bottomless pit and collected rock samples.

"Here you are, Garcia," the doctor said embarrassed, softer than his usual professional self, handing him a mug of tea. "About last night—the rum—shouldn't take these things so seriously, George."

What pleased George was being addressed as Garcia, even if the doctor had not got it clear in his own head. Even if it was Rowan who took the message to Garcia. But in *his* head George was clear about the incident—he was a Garcia. He was a general.

By the time they had reached town, he was stumbling with fatigue and unable to think or talk.

The doctor said good-bye to him at the cordial works where

86

he lived in a room at the back. The doctor patted his back and mumbled something.

Next day George sat mixing syrup, thinking about having made the moonlight clamber down the valley to fetch water that was not wanted. He did not feel in any way a fool, although it seemed from every side to have been a foolish thing to have done.

The whole thing had no purpose other than what he wanted to make of it.

He had gone on and done something in the face of the meaningless.

For all the meaninglessness, seemingly, George felt personally that he had accomplished *something*, even if it was not the fetching of the water, which was really only the surface of it all.

It was something like this. He had forced the meaninglessness of it to a bitter end. He had played it right out. He had been relentless. He had turned the absurdity of it on its own head.

If he had stopped short at any point it would have been absurd, but he'd taken the bait—and the rod.

It had a certain perfection to it.

His father called in and he told him of the events. His father laughed and said, "Maybe the doctor wanted a little quiet", referring to George's tendency to talk overlong.

No, he had played the absurdity of it, forced it right through. Acted it right out.

He'd been relentless.

George felt perfectly all right about it, went on with his work, fully occupied with his work, with no loose thoughts of unease about it at all.

He'd been relentless.

The Rotary Platform

(adopted 1911 Rotary Convention)

●

Recognizing the commercial basis of modern life as a necessary incident in human evolution, the Rotary Club is organized to express the proper relation between private interests and the fusion of private interests which constitute society.

To accomplish this purpose more effectively, the principle of limited membership has been adopted, the Rotary Club consisting of one representative from each distinct line of business or profession. Each member is benefited by contact with representative men engaged in different occupations and is enabled thereby to meet more intelligently the responsibilities of civic and business life.

The basis of club membership ensures the representation of all interests and the domination of none in the consideration of public questions relating to business. On account of its limited membership the Rotary Club does not constitute itself the voice of the entire community on questions of general importance, but its action on such questions is of great influence in advancing the civic and business welfare of the community.

The Rotary Club demands fair dealings, honest methods, and high standards in business. No obligation, actual or implied, to influence business exists in Rotary. Election to membership therein is an expression of confidence of the club in the member elected, and of its good will towards him. As his business is an expression of himself, he is expected actively to represent it.

Membership in the Rotary Club is a privilege and an opportunity and its responsibility demands honest and efficient service and thoughtfulness for one's fellows.

Service is the basis of all business.

He profits most who serves best.

Here's a Tip

•

A good pinch of bicarbonate soda will keep milk from going off when you haven't an ice-chest or are going on a picnic.

A Skin Bleach for Blackfellows

•

From a talk delivered to the Science Club in 1928 by John Brill, local pharmacist, titled, "Solving the Problem of Coloured Races".

Science can come to the aid of the blackfellow and many of them could become quite white if only they would make the effort. The following preparation is recommended. Take some Yellow Wax 8 ounces, Vaseline 8 ounces, Cocoa Butter 2 ounces. Melt these together in a double boiler. Take off the fire and add a solution of 10 grains of corrosive sublimate in one ounce of alcohol and pour into jars while warm. This may be used before retiring. First wash the face, neck and arms with a good soap and hot water. Rinse well and dry, then apply the cream. In the morning wash off and apply a good powder. Do this at least every other day.

THE
SECRET
OF
ENDURANCE

WITH Zane Grey he had not been at ease and had not, as far as he could see, derived that much—it was partly the fishing, he not being a fisherman as Zane Grey was, and also he'd been lost among the other tourists and what Zee Gee called his "fans" crowding about—despite his letter of introduction to Zee Gee—this changed later at the camp and he was recognized for what he was, a coastal Rotarian wanting to parley with another "achiever", although certainly their achievement lay in different paddocks—Zee Gee the writer and big-game fisherman and he a manufacturer—of aerated waters—still, the man's style charmed him and even the American manager chap Bowen, who, of course, had at first tried to fob him off, which was understandable with people coming over three hundred miles to see Zee Gee and crowding around, and the Americans could not be expected to have known him after only a few weeks on the coast, because of that, and having heard that Zee Gee was, like himself, a teetotaller, he presented him with a sample range of his aerated waters in way of a calling card—but the fishing was the thing that kept them apart, made the discussion he proposed in the letter—fusion of self and public interest—so difficult because of Zee Gee's single-mindedness about fishing and his introversion—all men are shy, but introversion was something else—but, still, about the wide-open spaces and reliance on self they could agree, although it had not been intended for discussion, but as a result of his unintended discussion he planned personally to lead a more outdoors life himself, not spend as much time in the smoke of meetings and more time in the cathedral of the bush, although one could lose sight that the "meeting" and the "committee" were two of man's supreme creations and the answer to Socialism—the meeting was the place where private will and public need were assembled and packed—where talk became motion—he always said the committee was a mill for raw ideas and that the country was really run by a thousand committees—he'd wanted to talk with Zee Gee about disinterested public effort, but they didn't get on to this—service above self—the death of King George that month shook the nation

95

and business—although he hadn't noticed any fall-off in the sale of bottled drinks—but the King's death may have contributed to the not altogether menti-cultural nature of the meeting, although again the death of King George seemed to matter nought to Zee Gee and his party with all their talk about trolling and light lead and heavy lead and revolving bait—use shark to catch shark—he felt uncomfortable there in the canvas chairs under the trees at Bermagui and later, too, when he visited again at Bateman's Bay camp, but camp in style they did! he granted them that, that was the American Way, a dozen tents or so brightly coloured, two professional cooks, a sit-down dining-room, and a benzine kitchen, that was camping in style—we must keep the open spaces and the natural life, Zee Gee said, not just parks but real open spaces without fences where a man can walk free—don't let them fence this country in—he replied to Zee Gee that Australians wanted roads before parks—"We have to tie ourselves together with roads," he said, being very "road-minded", still he saw what Zee Gee was saying about unfenced space—he was quite taken by the movie-making at the camp and got a kick out of hearing Bowen say through a megaphone, "Roll 'em", which it was explained was an order to the camera operators to start the electric motors which power the cameras —but he declined the invitation to invest in Zee Gee's film, though he heard later that others had—Zee Gee said Australia, he sensed, was a far country, one surrounded by vast oceans with something he could not give a name to "hanging over the country"—a poetic thing to say—he interposed, less poetically, that this was why Australians were "road-minded"— the need not *for space* but to overcome space—"You Australians do remarkably well with the wrong measures," Zee Gee said at another point referring, he took it, to the tackle but also to the wrongheadedness, as Zee Gee saw it, of many of the Australian ways of doing things—but he reminded Zee Gee wryly, without meaning to offend, that it was Dr Faithfull of Inverlocky Station who beat the American party to the first swordfish of the season—he, in fact, saw the head and bill at Lynch's Hotel on the way down—Zee Gee rose at

5 a.m., wrote for three hours and then fished in the "insatiate, crawling sea"—he himself did not have a recreation like Zee Gee but he was not altogether sure that this was necessarily a matter for self-disapproval, games were for the young and the old, the game of life was enough for him—in reply to a question about the Australian bush, Zee Gee said that at first the eucalyptus had "pasted closed his nostrils", a writer's way of saying things—"Call me Zee Gee," he said during the early stages of their discussion—"As long as you don't mind me calling you Zee Gee"—"No, call me Zee Gee"—Zee Gee then showed him how they had put floorboards in all the tents—they knew how to camp!—the party had been discouraged at first by the laughter of the jackass and had fired at them, but now they rather welcomed the morning and the evening laughter—"If you want to catch fish, you must keep your bait in the water," Zee Gee said to him on the subject of Perseverance—he thought, but did not say, that Perversity was not Perseverance and that a man should not hate what he hunts, having perceived in Zee Gee a hatred of the shark—sharks he quickly perceived were an obsession with him and probably also with Australians—Mr Stead, the expert on sharks from Sydney, had a daughter who published stories, but Zee Gee was interested only in talking about the sharks—Zee Gee said Australians got their bigness and their warmth from the Australian bush—again he could not fully agree, feeling neither big nor warm and feeling the bush to be neither big nor warm, and suggested, contrarily, that Australians got their insufficient confidence and fear of life from the fear of the bush and the fear of the shark—from living in a land surrounded by bush that stretches unendingly, growing up, as he had, surrounded by unexplored bush that stretched for thousands of miles, and surrounded by dangerous seas, and again he brought in the need for roads—Zee Gee continued on the theme of tenacity, saying that he fished for eighty-three days without a bite—tenacity, and perseverance, and then, lo! on the eighty-fourth day he caught the Tahitian Striped Marlin—he asked Zee Gee what had been the biggest disappointment in his life—Zee Gee answered: when the

writer Ernest Hemingway refused to fish with him, he had
said to Hemingway, "We are both writers and fishermen,
but you write better than I, and I fish better than you"—this
Ernest Hemingway had turned him down flat—he did not
know of this Ernest Hemingway and did not fully grasp the
disappointment involved in this for Zee Gee, but he always
asked that question of great men for what it might reveal—
Zee Gee caught the Leaping Green Fox Thresher Shark, the
first caught in Australian waters, but this too meant very
little to him—"I won't let the white death sharks lick me,"
Zee Gee said, again the hate of the shark—there'd been talk
of Tivoli show girls at the camp but he did not see any—apart
from fishing, Zee Gee did not seem to be a wastrel—"We must
preserve the uncultivated lands, the feeding and nesting
swamps," Zee Gee said—like Zee Gee, he supported the Boy
Scout movement because it taught the endurance of privation,
the endurance of pain, cultivated strength of body and sim-
plicity of mind—he wrote this down in his notes together
with Zee Gee's words, "We are driven to roam, hunt and
slay", but did not share the feeling behind these words—he
was not a roamer, nor a slayer: he was a stayer and a maker—
talking of roaming, Zee Gee said, "People travel not to look
and learn but to eat and drink", which he agreed with—on
the question Women Today, Zee Gee said the women of the
thirties resembled too much the male—the sexes were merging
—when are women going to look like women—on this George
did not agree, he did not mind shingled hair and liked women
to be independent-minded—Zee Gee said that on the matter
of sex confusion many of his thirteen million readers did not
know his sex and mistook his name for that of a woman,
regardless that he wrote of the wild west and self-reliant
men—he subscribed to the theory that men should teach
boys and women should teach girls—"The boy exists in me
always, nailed to the martyrdom of fishing"—he talked about
the cruelty of fishing to the body, the strain, the wet, the cold,
the need for manly strength, "I say—I endure because I am
a *fisherman*," Zee Gee said—in New Zealand, Zee Gee said,
returning to the problem of the merging of the sexes, many

said they thought he was a woman because of his name, which had very much upset him—I, on the other hand, thought George, I endure because I get off my backside and I bust my gut, I am in no way a fisherman and I have not learned very much at all from Great Men this year.

A Literary Coincidence

•

It is a literary coincidence that Zane Grey once went eighty-three days without a bite and then caught the Tahitian Striped Marlin and that the Old Man in Hemingway's *The Old Man and the Sea* went eighty-four days before catching his giant marlin.

A Home-made Cooling System

•

Procure a wire meat-safe—that is, a box with walls made of perforated metal, with a flyproof door. On top, place a pan filled with water. Take a piece of burlap the width of the safe and sufficient to wrap around the entire safe. Tack it fast where the door opens and closes. Tuck the upper edge in water. Place it where there is a draught and where the dripping will do no damage. This constitutes a well-ventilated refrigerator that costs nothing but the water to maintain.

THE
ANNUAL
CONFERENCE
OF 1930 AND
SOUTH COAST
DADA

THE turning of the screw, stopped by the words, "The world is a long journey, Mr McDowell." Scribner's head. Scribner bending down to see under the car, "Taking a journey, Mr McDowell?"

"The Annual Conference of the New South Wales Country Cordial Makers Association, Mr Scribner," he said from under the car, his voice cramped.

Scribner picked up and held an unnecessary spanner.

Scribner always made himself a part of the situation.

The screw turning completed.

He dragged himself out from under the car, "The world *is* a long journey," he said to Scribner.

Scribner always made himself a part of the situation and addressed himself to the situation.

He ingratiated himself by slicing, pouring, or serving.

Yet he belonged in no situation.

Slicing, pouring, serving, holding or assisting.

Scribner was also good at quotation, which pleased him because he liked to hear a good quotation.

Scribner said, "I myself have been considering a trip to the city to buy my summer underwear."

He dusted himself from being under the car and thought that he did not vary *his* underwear year-long. Why then did Scribner vary his underwear? And why buy it in the city? Was it education or was it because he and his mother considered themselves "above the town".

He found himself quite easily saying, yes, that today he would not mind the company of Scribner.

On some days he could not abide the idleness of Scribner or his wandering, picnicking conversation.

He liked Scribner when he felt in a truant mood. He usually fought against this truancy in himself, but yet it did relax him—when he allowed himself to go like a balloon in the breeze. Babbling on with fantasy and speculation.

Being above the town did not save Scribner from being known as a glutton. His mother also, it was said, looked after herself at town functions.

"I was reading only yesterday," said Scribner, "talking of cordials—about the brewing of barley beer in Mesopotamia—they kept their brewing recipes secret. O they valued alcohol highly in ancient times."

"And today also, Mr Scribner."

"Yes, and today also, Mr McDowell."

Some in the town had wanted him to go into brewing, but he had decided to go the other way and stay in "temperance drinks"—aerated waters and maybe egg drinks and milk drinks, which he thought had a future when there was more refrigeration.

"Above the town", but the Scribners, mother and son, never missed a town function invited or not, nor missed a sandwich, a sausage roll, a piece of sponge cake, a pikelet, a cup cake, a scone, a trifle.

Being a Bachelor of Arts was why he supposed that no one minded that Scribner belonged in no situation, did not work at a job. Although he did write letters to Government Departments for those people worried about the right way of doing so.

And Scribner was a speechmaker, invited or not, and always used a Latin line, which he liked, and had enough sense to explain it without implying that you did not know.

Of course, people said, and it was probably so, that the Scribners, mother and son, had little money. That explained, people said, why they ate the way they did at every town function. For a long time it was said that the Scribners had shares, but maybe the Depression had rendered these valueless.

It seemed to answer why they stuffed themselves at every town function.

Scribner made the occasional guinea by writing an advertisement for him, but always took the money offered in payment as some unexpected, though welcome, consideration.

"Isn't there anything you wish to collect from your house before we set off, Mr Scribner? Your valise?"

Scribner said, no, he could go as he was and perhaps buy a toothbrush and toothpowder and stay at the Masonic Club.

He lent Scribner an old dustcoat for the journey up the coast.

"Who told you I was planning a trip to the city, Mr Scribner?"

"O I came across you simply by chance, Mr McDowell. I was taking a stroll."

That was the whole damn' difference between himself and Scribner. Scribner daily placed himself in the hands of fate. He, on the other hand, worked at making fate do what he wanted. The whole damn' difference.

Yet here they were, in the same car, going to the same destination.

Scribner, he was sure, did not know from day to day his income or even his possible whereabouts. Except that if the town had a banquet, a ball, a garden party, dinner, reception, afternoon tea, Scribners, mother and son, would appear and Scribner would, unsolicited, begin to pour, slice, or serve. They belonged to no local organization. Or did they consider themselves members of every organization ex-officio?

The town's social calendar guided Scribner through life. He, on the other hand, organized the social calendar.

Scribner asked about the Cordial Makers Association, saying, "I always believed that 'two of a trade did never agree'."

"Hard times have hurt the Association, but we've agreed on standards. I've opposed Major Adcock's move to put a Jusfrute Factory in every town. Wanted the Association to oppose this. I'm for every town having its distinctive local products."

He then asked Scribner if he worried for the future, given his style of life.

Scribner replied that he sometimes felt himself to be the embodiment of the Greek god Perseus.

"Which was he, Mr Scribner?"

"Perseus—as though I have the helmet of Pluto which makes me invisible. O everyone expects me to be where I am and no longer notices me. Therefore I am invisible. O and the wings of Hermes because I move where I want and there is always a way—today, thanks to your fine motor-car, Mr McDowell—" Scribner patted the dashboard—"and the

Mirror of Athene, which permits me to avoid looking into the dangerous gaze of Mammon or the snakepit called the Opinions of Others, and so I avoid the anxieties of life."

Scribner, some said, was also close to being mad.

He liked Scribner for talking in an educated fashion and he, himself, found that he talked in a more elevated way when with Scribner.

Both sat over the dusty miles in their dustcoats.

"It has always struck me, Mr Scribner, that as an educated man you could have done more with your talents."

"What more could I offer life, Mr McDowell? Why I have written a number of immortal labels for your aerated waters!"

It was true that Scribner could always find a new word for "refreshing" and could tread the difficult line between a "fancy" invented name and a simple descriptive name and yet still get registration. All Scribner's names for new lines had gained registration. The last had been "Green River" for the lime.

"One day, Mr McDowell, the label, the advertisement, will be considered works of art. O yes, demeaned today, but in the future—say in 1950 or 1960 when people fully understand the meaning of Art—I predict that they will be considered the Art of Our Times. The embodiment of our Dreams."

"You think so, Mr Scribner—that advertising could be, for instance, the poetry of commerce?"

"Indeed, I do. And the machines we use—the sculptures of industry."

That was a tickling idea.

"Some of the French already do, Mr McDowell. I myself am a French Futurist in Art. Yes, indeed. We wrap our life in words, Mr McDowell. Our poor mundane daily existence would be nothing without the illusions we weave about them. Illusions, Mr McDowell, are the game we play with our selves and life. Words are the 'Sparkling Juices from the Fountain of Delight'."

"That was one of your best, Mr Scribner."

"Thank you, Mr McDowell."

"Unfortunately, isn't it true that once you recognize these illusions, as you call them, once you see it is a 'game', Mr Scribner, don't they disappear? Is that not the case?"

"A painful philosophical truth, painfully true."

He raised with Scribner his own belief in the "speech" and the "business letter" as the practical arts of commerce.

"Noble arts, Mr McDowell, with a long tradition— 'When he killed a calf he would do it in high style and make a speech.' Why, you're a Futurist yourself, Mr McDowell."

He told Scribner he did not know about that, but he was against the trend to shorter speeches.

Scribner said with great feeling and some emotion, and not altogether to the point, that the Letter was a failed form. "We taught the People to write and they never made anything of the Letter. I have read many attempts at the Letter. The greatest condemnation of Mass Literacy has been the failure of the People to produce Great Letters. The Letter to the Editor is also a failed form."

Scribner was spluttering and salivating with feeling for his words.

"The telephone has harmed the letter, don't you think, Mr Scribner?"

"Ah, but then we must make the telephone the instrument of Art. The Telephonic Essay."

"I myself plan out each Telephonic Conversation."

"That is a credit to you, Mr McDowell, but we must not undervalue the spontaneous, the ephemeral, the extemporaneous. Why don't People take delight? Why! the Telephonic Essay is one of the great extemporaneous arts. There is, Mr McDowell. . . ."

Scribner was spluttering off again with great gusto for his words. ". . . the art, Mr McDowell, which comes from striving, practice, revision and attachment to the traditions—poetry, painting and so forth—and there is the art which comes from felicitous practice in the daily run of our lives."

Scribner wiped his mouth with his handkerchief. "But we don't, but we don't become artists without an act of conscious dedication. No, no, no, there must be dedication to the Muse, dedication of one's Spirit to the idea of doing things super-latively. A dedication to the superlative. And the painstaking accumulation of the supporting skills."

Scribner fell into exhausted silence, cooling himself by flapping his silk handkerchief, wiping his face, dabbing his neck. He seemed to carry more than one handkerchief.

"I consider yourself to be so dedicated, Mr McDowell," Scribner managed to get out.

"Thank you, Mr Scribner."

When he had recovered himself a few miles farther on, Scribner launched off again, saying, "I consider myself a Dadaist and of the Bohemian Tradition, but I salute you as a Business-man Artist."

They had passed through the heavy, foreboding bush that closed in on the narrow road between Milton and Nowra, through which they sat silent, inturned, in the cold darkness of the overshadowed road. They grinned and talked a lot when they were out of it and into the open valleys of Berry and Gerringong. It was a relief to see the sea from time to time. Although they could not be lost, there was no way of being lost really, it was good to be sure. They then hugged the embankment around the winding spurs of Kiama, looked and spoke, as everyone did, of the convict fences of the English fields around Kiama.

They were again silent through the tar roads of Wollongong, knowing at that point they had left well and truly behind the outer limits of the district in which they might be known. He did not care for the larger towns where there were more people who did not know you than people who knew you.

"It is a lonely and unrewarding life being the only Dadaist on the coast, Mr McDowell."

The other side of Wollongong the front tyre was punctured by a piece of broken horseshoe. They lunched at the tearooms at Bulli before trying the Pass and going back into the dark, empty bush before Sydney.

Scribner ordered double servings and blew his nose while the bill was being paid.

As they whined and chugged up Bulli Pass, he joked to

Scribner that they were certainly not "Hope Bartletts" and the Chev was no racing-car. He asked Scribner how one became a Business-man Artist, in his opinion. He did not ask about how one became a Dadaist.

"What is needed, Mr McDowell," he said, above the motor, "is to have once *thought the thought*—about striving for the superlative. That's enough, to have *thought the thought*. To have *thought the thought*, understood it, cherished it, as an ideal. Of course, it cannot remain in the forefront of your mind for long, but to have *thought the thought* means that you are then servant of the thought. Some thoughts, you see, contain imperatives and instructions, and once you have had them pass through your head, they affect the spirit. They leave behind instructions to be followed. Some thinking permits of no retreat. One cannot go back, Mr McDowell, to what one was before having come across the thought and allowed it to pass into the mind. Not all thoughts, just some thoughts. We never please an Ideal, Mr McDowell. O no. O no. O Idealism is a taskmaster, Mr McDowell, who makes us permanently dissatisfied with our self."

He nodded at Scribner's words, trying to keep his own thoughts out of the way so he could fully listen.

"Not a happy state, Mr McDowell."

"No."

He had never heard these sorts of thoughts said before. He marvelled that a man like Scribner, who daily placed himself in the hands of fate and did not have goals and plans, should have such ideas. It convinced him that the town was wrong when it thought Scribner a joking matter, which some did, despite his Bachelor's Degree.

He then told Scribner that although the words just spoken were new to him, he had felt similar things. He found that in the town there were too few who could go along with such types of thinking.

"They do not make the conversational possibilities—they keep certain doors closed. Do you know what I mean, Mr Scribner? They do not allow certain thinking to come out because of their tightly closed demeanour. The ideas in one's head become shy and wary. Some people frighten ideas away. And words from your mouth."

"I am an enemy of those who frighten away my words and ideas, Mr McDowell," Scribner said with vehemence, hostility.

"I'm afraid there are some in the Science Club even, who by their general demeanour stop the ideas dead in your head. I must say, Mr Scribner, I find that my ideas are enthusiastic to meet yours."

"I wish I were more a man of affairs sometimes, like yourself, Mr McDowell."

"But you are a Bachelor of Arts."

"All mysteries, Mr McDowell, find their resolution in human practice. A student only lists and classifies the mysteries. Karl Marx, ogre of our Times, said that."

"Even Mr Marx, then, knows something. They say, I believe, that truth is dispersed among us."

"But not equally, Mr McDowell. Believe me, in all humility, some of us have more than others. Believe me."

Although there was little talk over the last miles, Scribner burst out at Sutherland, saying, "No, damn it, I am not a Dadaist. No, I am not. I am an Everydayist. I believe in the ultimate beauty of everyday things. I'm no Dadaist."

He did not question Scribner about this or what he meant by it. It was, it seemed, a private tussle. He had feared through the journey the word "Dadaist". Not having understood it. He had understood and heard enough for the one day. He did not care to venture further than he had in the conversation. He did not want to ask about the word "Dadaist", because he did not know what lay behind it. He doubted that Scribner, anyhow, belonged to any of these organizations he mentioned.

His mind, also, was turning to tomorrow, the city, and the Annual Conference.

At Kogarah they stopped and removed their dustcoats and washed their hands in the park, before driving into the city. Scribner went over and stole a flower from a garden in a nearby house, called Denbigh, and put the flower in his buttonhole. This act of theft filled him with apprehension.

Annoyed, he refused to accept the buttonhole flower Scribner had stolen for him.

That had been the only irritation of the journey.

Since he was staying at Adams' Tattersalls, he dropped Scribner at the Masonic Club.

"It's good afternoon, or should I say evening, then, Mr Scribner."

"Yes, and a good evening to you, Mr McDowell. My regards to the cordial-makers of this State. Good conferencing and all that. Conference, they say, maketh a ready man."

He noticed to his surprise that although Scribner was not a Mason, the doorman at the club knew him and tipped his cap.

Extraordinary.

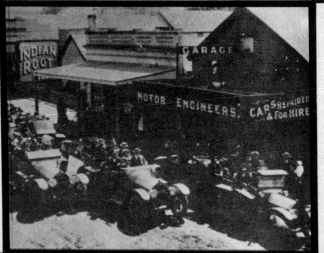

An Interesting Point

•

When Frank Fowler rang long distance from Melbourne to
wish the Conference all best wishes, it was George's idea for all
those present to sing "For he's a Jolly Good Fellow" to Frank,
over the telephone.

Aerated Waters—
Some Technical Considerations

•

1. Natural juices and squashes do not produce a natural, convincing colour—the question of tinting and keeping the tint consistent from bottle to bottle is important. People suspect quality if the colour varies.

2. Sighting—the inspection of bottles before filling is of prime importance. One dirty bottle or one bottle containing a foreign substance can destroy your business. Inspection is tedious. Change your employees around, giving them each a turn at inspection and never one person longer than a couple of hours.

3. Your reputation is behind the name on your bottle. Watch out for Soda Fountain operators who illegally refill bottles branded with your name.

4. The word squash or crush must not be misused—it should be the juice of sound fruit with no added pulp or other substance, except for sugar and preservative.

5. Most town water-supplies are not pure enough for bottling of drinks. Organisms can cause ropiness. Settling tanks and filters keep the water free of dust and germs.

6. Most breakages occur because of bad boxes—keep them repaired.

TELL CHURCHILL THAT T. GEORGE McDOWELL IS ON HIS FEET

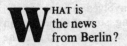

WHAT is the news from Berlin?

What is the news from Paris. London? Just how does one know what is really happening. Who to ask. On what does one construct one's actions in these times of allegation.

Where are the Rules of Conduct.

Dr Russell, a West End neurologist, said recently that the child of the thirties is already "out of hand". He attributes this to too much reading of books and attendance at moving pictures in cinemas. By the time the child is twelve, more experience and sights have passed through the child's brain than would have passed through the brain of a man in a lifetime previously. The brain wore out in the child's head.

Was this, in fact, correct?

Was electric light the unnatural extension of daylight?

When he had been younger he had not doubted. But it had been an illusion of certainty when young. As if certainty and ignorance were closely related. There seemed now to be too much information, but yet, however, just not enough. You put together a decision and "made up" your mind, when along came some fellow in a newspaper with "fresh facts" and "startling discoveries" and you were back where you began.

He could remember arguing the merits of benzine against kerosene. For why?

How did one ascertain true facts?

He stared down at the *Sydney Morning Herald*, and many voices spoke to him from many written pieces, all with equal confidence. Who were these Special Correspondents? One man?

Does one always have to find one's way through life in peril of being wrong?

He could not bear the waste of life involved in being wrong. They say that someone has to be wrong, so that someone can be right. That someone has to test the wrong way, so that the right way can be found.

Then why weren't those who were wrong also rewarded?

It seemed until now, this night, he had been a man of certainty. He could not now find the requisite number of facts.

Who cared whether benzine from petroleum was superior to kerosene from shale oil.

They say that too many bad decisions on matters such as benzine *v.* kerosene and refrigeration *v.* ice led to starvation of the race, the downfalling of culture, return of the savage, civilization into a backwater, the failure of the harvest.

Do we approach perfection? Or is every generation confronted with an equal number of problems? Different problems but still as many—still to be solved by men of action.

Do all solutions reveal an equal number of new complications?

The solution of the problem of flight created the problems of air navigation, the need for the parachute.

We think we progress because we know the answers to yesterday's problems.

Do all solutions, maybe, create even greater complexities? Are humans, in fact, bunglers? Is civilization a bungle? Will we soon reach the Perfect Problem and not the Perfect Answer? The Insoluble?

What would the world be like in 1950?

Of all the women who crossed one's path, how had he chosen Thelma? On what basis?

Of all the occupations, trades and professions, on what basis had he chosen aerated water and cordial manufacturing? What had been the guiding magnetism?

I do not know. I do not now know.

He was not ready, though, to believe in a god. Sensible men are all of the same religion. But now, when he went through the names and faces of his friends and business associates, he could not decide which were sensible and which were not.

I try to walk the footpath of goodwill.

Isn't that enough?

He sat before a shaded desk-light in his office. The centre of his life. All he ever wanted from life had been "an office". An office of his own from which to control his life and works. His rank and his position. The staff had gone home. The factory creaked and the machinery made cooling and settling noises after the heat and running of the day. He owned it, yet the noises of the empty factory sometimes made him frightened and alert.

He had talked to the Science Club some years back about O. C. Overbeck's theories that electricity would cure illness. How did he know that? How could he have spoken with such confidence then? How could someone like him in a country town know that O. C. Overbeck's theories were correct or not? How would he know whether the body was electrical and that illness was no more than a disturbance of the electric balance between negative and positive within the brain, that new cells generated electricity which became energy, that defective vision could be corrected by introducing electrical current into the brain, that the fibrils of the body were nothing more than electric wires? That acute depression could be cured by electric current? How could he have stood up before the Science Club and said that? What had the doctor thought? Shame burned in him for his youth.

He had no degree. Once it had not worried him at all. Now he would dearly love to be a Bachelor of Arts or a Bachelor of Science.

He had been a real magsman in his day. Nothing more than a magsman.

Behind every word and every object lay knowledge which he did not have. Behind every leaf of nature, mechanism of life, trick of fate, lay knowledge he did not have.

He wanted dearly to be, say, a Master of Arts or a Doctor of Philosophy and be privy to the secrets in them contained.

What for instance was happening in Germany?

What was the news from Berlin?

When you lived in a town on the coast of Australia, how did you find out what was happening in private rooms and secret conferences in London, in Paris, and in Berlin?

Why would they tell George McDowell?

Did one choose a creed to carry one through one man's lifetime—caterpillar tracks to take one over those questions which could not be answered?

Why did the highly educated disagree among themselves? He could not fathom that.

Could one live without faith, live with the insoluble, unanswerable, unknowable, the untrustworthy, poor tradesmanship, back-biting, and the enclosing blackness?

What to answer his children? What if one generation had no answers for the generation which followed it?

Did the Rosicrucians know the secrets?

The Masons didn't. He knew that.

How did one group of people in life come by the Secrets and not everyone else?

Pelmanism?

He always said there were rules inherent in one's craft.

But one rule inherent in all crafts is the obligation, the exhortation, the stricture, to improve one's techniques, tools, to find the best way, to deliver the goods, and to perceive the ethics inherent, the way the craft was meant to serve the tribe.

He always said one worked not only with materials, but through the materials with people. What you made with your hands and offered to people was your gesture to people and the presentation of yourself.

Now all this did not answer him. It plagued him. How to perceive and interpret. What to change and what to leave untouched.

The making of foodstuffs was the most sacred of all crafts.

Even if it was only soft drinks.

He'd always believed that the Rules of Conduct grew outward from the rules inherent in one's work. He believed that general theories which grew from so-called "theorists", and not from practice and work, were dangerous. If only all people obeyed the Rules of Conduct inherent in their work.

He could no longer perceive the Rules of Conduct.

One moved from birth, it seemed, shaped and directed by others, to the making of decisions of minor importance which followed daily, one upon the other, until unnoticed they were decisions of importance about other people and you were then in full flood of decision, each built one on the other, until, viewed from Life's Lookout, they appeared as a terrifying torrent with uncontrollable consequence.

Where were the answers he once lived by—where had they gone?

He voted on everything: he had never abstained from life's decisions.

A newspaper reporter like Backhouse never voted.

Tutman was dead.

Backhouse knew the rules inherent in his craft. He simply had to print. The rest was up to those out in the world of meetings.

The World of Meetings.

Was there a rapid increase in sickness and more madness? Or was this scare talk?

Were men becoming more like women and women more like men? Zane Grey certainly thought so. It could be that there were too many women schoolteachers. How to know?

Who had stolen his leather coat?

Now that he had possessions and success, people stole from him, talked about him behind his back, tried to befriend him falsely.

Fred had rigged up an improvement for labelling, and the man doing the bottle-washing had sneered at him saying, "You'll get on." He had overheard this. He did not sack the bottle-washer, he lectured him. Lecturing improved a man, sacking never did. He told him that he had no time for those who tried to hold others back. Australia was pinned down and kicked in the head by expressions like "She'll be right", "Near enough", or "Don't bust your gut", or "Leave it to George."

Busting your gut was what life was all about.

Resentment of ability. Now he was for ever on guard against trickery, theft in the factory, false representation, flattery, and borrowers.

The trouble with the Unions and the Public Service was that they were making it impossible to work hard any more.

A person *should* be tired after a day's work. For god's sake.

Now someone had taken his leather coat.

It seemed that as public recognition grew, so did the private resentment. He'd noticed it against himself. That often those who gave the public recognition—made the speeches, moved the votes of thanks, nominated you for office—were also the people who resented, often saying the reverse of what they felt, and the opposite of what they said in private.

He liked to mix now only with successful men.

124

Where was the religion for the strong and successful? They need comfort as much as the humble and weak.

I am assailed.

The supernatural was the natural not yet explained.

But what to do in the meantime?

I believe only in the work I do.

Gwen was ten and another child expected. He had bought for Gwen, and the child expected, a horse, a cow, a goat, a pig, and a dog. He wanted them to know that we ultimately depend on animals and the things of nature. Or was this a form of madness?

The Royal Arch—trowel, sword and buckler—ineffable name and ineffable triangle.

Why did he go on with the humbug of Masonry.

I provide for myself and family and more. Through my ideas and management others have work to do. What more is asked of me?

He knew the arguments against carbonated drinks—that carbonated drinks retarded the digestion by interfering with the salivary glands. The Australian Wine, Brewing, Spirit and Aerated Waters Review had refuted this.

He pulped his own fruit and made his own essence. Except for the lime drink, Green River. He triple-filtered his water.

Business was not "organized greed", it was the joining of skills of many men to one man's ideas.

He had started kiosks on three beaches. He believed in kiosks.

He ran a good business. Didn't that count for anything? No one thanked him.

Someone had stolen his leather coat.

Tears came to his eyes but did not fall.

He could not go on.

His leather coat.

There was no longer any point. He lacked certitude. Backhouse could publish in his newspaper that T. George McDowell had come to a dead stop.

T. George McDowell could not go on.

T. George McDowell was sorry.

A long silence came to his head.

No thought came.

The creaking of the factory no longer frightened.

The tears did not leave his eyes, but his eyes stayed moist.

Spittle from his mouth.

The ring of the telephone.

The ring of the telephone.

He looked across to the telephone on the wall which had rung.

He stood up, his ears still holding the ringing of the telephone bell, and then went over and took the earpiece.

George?

We are waiting for you, George.

The meeting is waiting for you, George.

The meeting.

The meeting.

The Emergency Service Scheme—the motor unit.

O yes.

The car club.

Yes, the meeting.

George, are you all right?

George, we can't start without you.

The meeting.

Yes, I'm all right.

Yes, I'll be along.

Yes.

He hung up the telephone. Oh well, he was going on, he was keeping on. War was imminent, and they had to take some local initiative. The motor unit of civilian lorries and cars was his idea. Back Churchill. Sack Chamberlain.

His life was a walk between meetings.

This was the first time he had forgotten a meeting in his life. He had never left a door unlocked or forgotten a meeting.

It was a stumble, not a fall.

He was on his feet.

You can tell Churchill that T. George McDowell is on his feet.

He washed his face. As he did, a speech began to form in his mind. . . .

Problems Facing the Milk-shake
1938

•

While no one can deny the success of the milk-shake, it did have its problems.

—more women than men drank milk-shakes, because men considered it unmasculine to drink milk.

—some people couldn't drink whole milk (George overcame this for a while at the kiosks by offering a soda milk-shake consisting of soda-water and milk, but it was not overly popular).

—unrefrigerated milk often made people sick and gave the drink a bad name. Unrefrigerated milk also would not whip properly.

—some cafés did not think the electric mixer justified expense.

How to Mix a Milk-shake When You Do Not Have an Electric Mixer or Refrigeration

•

Put the milk, syrup, malt and a third of a tumbler of crushed ice into a shaker. Shake vigorously for a few minutes and then strain into a Parfait or Knickerbocker Glory glass.

THE
ST LOUIS
ROTARY
CONVENTION
1923,
RECALLED

B ECKER Meets the Kook

Becker was thinking this: how rarely in this foul country did the milk-carton spout open as the printed directions promised, "To open, push up here"—push up where, for goddam. It had to do with the spread of talent across the land. For a country with a population so small they should, in terms of technology, still be peasants. That was his feeling, harsh as it may be. The way he figured it, the high-performance five-percenters were spread over too diversified an economy. By accident of history. The accident of history being that they were English-speakers. They attempted the higher technology of the main English nations. That was it. Result: milk cartons which wouldn't spout.

Some theory, Becker, you could go back to the Alma Mater in Atlanta and package that into a Ph.D.

Of course, it explained his presence in the foul country. "To the foul country," he toasted with the milk carton, drinking through a jagged spout torn with his envelope-opening dagger. He was there to reinforce the top echelon of the country's paltry beverage technology—"to advise and counsel the franchise men in marketing".

"Here's to you, technological missonary, evangelist, old dog." He was, and he often thought it, he was an evangelist of sorts. The Peace Corps sort: he really sometimes feared that he had the Peace Corps mentality. But the corps never seemed to him to be the classic bourbon-drinking type of organization. And, he was the classic bourbon-drinking type.

The felt-penned drawing on a large sheet of pasteboard came down before him on the desk from behind, covering his hands and milk—as though he'd lost his hands to mid forearm in some disappearing act.

The relief secretary from the agency was standing there. He was unnerved. She herself had an uncertainty in her smile, her stance. She was waiting for him to put *her* at ease. Who would ease him?

"That me?" he asked, referring to the drawing.

"Yes, do you like it?"

Becker often felt that not a day went past when someone didn't inflict some extraordinary demand upon him way beyond what he felt should be expected of him in his job at Coca-Cola or of his guarded, programmed, elementary motel life. More, in fact, than he thought life itself had any right to throw up. He had not begun life visualizing, encompassing such things. Nor was he equipped or adequately trained. They are tests, Becker, tests. Yes, but tests for what? Where was the diploma, where was the payout?

"Well, do you like it?"

He'd been staring at the drawing—the caricature, obviously, of him.

"What am I doing with my hand shading my eyes?"

"You're searching."

"Searching?"

"New horizons."

O.K., he would pursue her meaning. He wanted in life to reduce enigmas. Back to the drawing. What he feared was that she was going to "reveal" him for what he was.

"New horizons?"

"New horizons for Coca-Cola. Or yourself?"

Well, that was damned true. "What's the Coke bottle doing on my head like some William Tell apple?"

"You have it on the brain—you're a Coke head." She giggled. "What's your star? Let me tell you . . . you're. . . ." She hummed and ha'd, staring into his eyes until not blinking strained him. "You're Pisces—sensitive, unlucky, and melancholy."

"You're damned right—about the star, that is." Further unnerved. "Say, how did you know that?"

"I knew." She gave off noises of self-congratulation.

"You looked up my personnel card?" he said. "And anyhow—changing the subject swiftly—is Coca-Cola subsidizing art now—or don't we give you enough to do?" Becker, wielder of the corporate inflation axe, pruner of manpower wastage.

"I did it in my lunch hour. Don't be mean."

"It's kookie—but I like it."

Becker worried that Sam would come out and see the drawing. Sam would show it to the others and they'd all have a great hee-haw. He didn't care for that.

Her name? "You're . . . ?" He snapped his fingers. But she left him hanging there, pinned there, endeavouring to remember, just too long for politeness, for social facility, just too long, and he sensed she liked, he bet, she liked to see men sweat. A Western Union thought arrived also: the drawing was a pass. There was a rule, he recalled, about fraternizing with female office staff. Perhaps that applied in Atlanta and not here.

"I'm Terri."

"Becker."

"I know—we've met before."

Sunburst Symbols, High signs, Hashbag

Her flat asked too much for Becker's liking. Not that he objected to art. Or fad art. But he found that he was most at ease in an electronic, twenty-four-hour, functional motel. Nothing talking back at you. In Terri's place everything was talking at you. Everything she'd done to the place was a message. From the time he stepped in, he was warding them off. The pottery, the artefacts, the prints, the posters, the sketches, the photographs, the pinned-up clippings, the dyed drapes, the books, were all like yelping dogs or crying children. Sunburst symbols, assorted carved statuettes from the East, high signs, and a hashbag hung from a small hookah.

"What's that burning?"

"Ethiopian sandalwood—incense."

"Uh, uh."

She went about doing things in another room. Motels. Now a motel was five-star living. Bourbon, a jar of hot mix, of which he was inordinately fond, a prewar movie or perhaps a Dashiell Hammett. Cleanliness, air-conditioning, refrigeration, comfort, nothing working away at your brain. Motels kept him a today-man because there was no yesterday around in a motel. Yesterday held you back.

"Say, you must be an artist," he said, catching her signature on some of the paintings.

"I did a course," she said. "I'm really only a passable sketcher, that's all—nothing more."

"Impresses a cowboy like me."

"Are you really a cowboy . . . I mean from Texas or somewhere?" she said, her words muffled by the sweater she was pulling over her head. He could see her bare back through in the bedroom.

"I sometimes see myself as a motel cowboy—making camp, riding on," he said, "but, no, I'm strictly city."

"How disappointing that you're not a real cowboy, not that I mean to be rude and not, of course, that they exist," she said with a rushed laugh. "I suppose I mean I haven't met anyone who comes from a backwoods way of life or something."

"No offence taken."

"You're going to my home town next week," she said, back in the living-room, handing him a drink, apologizing because she had no pot.

"Is that a prediction of the stars?"

"No." She laughed. "I was typing your itinerary."

Sam, please, not the rural parts. Becker, the motel cowboy, painfully rides his itinerary into the setting sun.

"Oh, where's your home town?"

She rattled on about it. How she hated it. How her father was a big shot.

King of Jasmine, Speed Freak

As he was taking off his trousers, he said, "I shouldn't be doing this.—I think it's against company rules."

"You don't really allow them to tell you who you go to bed with?"

"I try to keep the contract." Of which Becker had his own private interpretations.

"You're a victim."

"I keep the contract—I contracted in."

136

"But it's a matter of personal freedom . . . and control of your own work scene. I only work when I want to."

Becker didn't know precisely what she was on about. He didn't do anything else but work.

He kissed her. "I'm here, aren't I?"

In the bedroom she had King of Jasmine burning.

"I've never seen a man, a young man, wearing suspenders with his socks. Only my dad."

They lay on the bed.

"Some socks need suspenders."

"Aren't you going to take off your underpants, and your socks?"

"I thought we'd lie here for a while, kind of talk, finish our drinks. Can't rush a rabbit."

He held his drink to his lips with both hands. He studied the black and white print of the Archfiend in Goat Form with the Satanic curse, "Palas aron Azinomas".

A voice, which he took to be Godly, called to him, Becker what are you doing. He shook his head.

"Why are you shaking your head?"

"I was shaking my head?"

"You clown." She kissed him, and sat back, cross-legged, on the bed, naked, staring at him. "I like you."

He attempted a lying-down shrug. "I'm grey-flannel commerce. You're the radical, free spirit."

"I know . . . that's why I shouldn't like you . . . and American . . . I don't like Americans theoretically . . . but I do, you're my sort of person."

Jesus!

"I want an opinion," she said impulsively, rolling sideways off the bed, saying, "What do you think of a father who writes this sort of letter?" She went to the dresser.

Why me? Why Becker?

He put a hand to his face, two comforting fingers on his heavy eyelids making him see warm-pink.

Why.

"It's supposed to be personal, but he dictates to his secretary and it has a file number. I'll read the best parts."

She read: "Our dear Terri, Your mother and I were dreadfully disturbed to learn of your 'illness' ('he's put illness in quotation marks, Fowler says that's disowning the word, doesn't he?') but are relieved to know that it is now behind you and you have sought medical assistance. Many of these sorts of troubles are purely physical or a matter of resolve, of will. I have enclosed an article on the subject from a recent issue of the *Reader's Digest.* . . ."

Why me?

"In my own life I have always placed the greatest value on fellowship, on ethics, and on making one's own life secure ('he means making money', she interpolated). I hope this upbringing will eventually pay dividends ('for whom', Terri asked)."

Why?

"The incident you so painfully bring up had all but been forgotten by me, and I see no reason or purpose in you raising it again or telling it to the psychiatrist. I feel these childish acts are best kept within the family. Our thoughts are with you."

She threw the letter back onto the dressing-table. "Keep it within the family," she screamed, laughing. "Isn't that too much? He wants me to conceal things from the psychiatrist."

"You go to an analyst?" Becker asked.

"I did. I stopped."

Why me?

"Can you guess what the 'illness' was?"

Becker didn't want to try. People always asked you to guess the unguessable. He had a personal policy of not trying to guess. To guess anything. Why did people always want him to guess? No, he wasn't going to guess.

"You tell me."

"No. Guess."

"I couldn't guess. I don't want to guess."

The guessing challenge side-stepped, Terri was all too damned eager to tell.

"I had a crack-up . . . really freaked out on speed . . . an incredibly bad scene . . . raving, and they put me in security

138

with bars on the windows . . . where they put the real maddies and the 'bad' patients . . . they didn't treat me . . . just locked me away . . . and I looked out on a courtyard where all the maddies and morons walked about tearing off their clothes and eating their own shit . . . and when they undressed me, I bit two male nurses on the legs . . . is that significant . . .? then they gave me a canvas nightshirt and put me in this cell . . . it was a real cell and I pulled the bed apart to make a key . . . I don't know why I thought I could make a key from the bed . . . and they took the bed away and made me sleep on the cement floor on strips of canvas. . . ."

"Hey now, wait on, you don't expect me to believe this happened in these times. Why that's positively mediaeval."

Before his very eyes the kookie but swinging girl from work had become a neurotic problem. Sexually he began packing up. After keeping himself afloat in life, he didn't have enough left over.

"I'm not," she said, begging belief, "and my parents knew what was happening to me . . . and they let them do it . . . as punishment for me being sick."

"How long did they keep you in this . . . hospital?"

"Fifteen days."

"No!" Becker was truly shocked, wondering whether to believe it all.

"I was locked in this cell for fifteen days. Afterwards. I was put in an ordinary ward, where I got off with a fifty-year-old alcoholic under the hospital on some old bags, in the foundations. You could hear the people walking on the floor above. . . ."

"Spare me the details," Becker said.

". . . we took librium to get high . . . 10 mg. tablets. I took a bottle one day and they put me in the cell again for punishment—for another two days—and this time they shaved my head."

"No, they didn't shave your head. Terri that's not credible."

Becker found he'd sat up and was staring at the girl. She was speaking in a torrent.

She gulped her drink.

"Well, not shaved . . . but cropped. . . . They said there was a lice infestation."

Lice was one of the things Becker had not had to face in life. He was not going to face lice now.

"They discharged me to my parents, and as soon as I arrived home I took a bottle of chloral hydrate and a packet of those tranquilizers you get from the chemists without prescription . . . and they put me back in hospital."

Becker wondered how to get out without hurting her and whether there was anything Coca-Cola could do to help. Whether there was the remotest possibility she had lice. Now.

"The reason people are down on drugs is they resent people escaping and having an easily gotten good time. I'm no addict. I was just having a bad scene with a guy and wanted to be out of the world for a while. Do you know what the 'painful incident' was? The one my father would rather I didn't mention."

"No," said Becker, not wanting to know, not wanting to know a further damned item.

"It was during my 'active phase', as the shrink calls it . . . when I was younger. I stripped naked and got into bed with my father while he was asleep and slashed him with a razor-blade . . . not badly . . . just superficial cuts. . . . Is that castration?"

"Just superficial cuts, uh?" Becker said, nodding. Becker knew nothing of castration and was having none of it. None.

Protesting a backache, he proceeded to remove himself from the situation.

"You mean you've been kissing and we're undressed and now you're going to go without making love to me?"

She seemed not to believe that he could go. He was sure he could.

"You think I'm mad, don't you?" she cried, complaining, wanting, he could tell, for him to say no. Which he couldn't.

"I'm concerned, Terri . . . maybe, I thought . . . maybe the office might be able to . . . a lot of people don't realize how good Coca-Cola is about these . . . things." He too had his doubts.

"You're too much," she said nastily, and began to laugh in a way which was like sobbing, which caused Becker to look again. Naked, she was laughing at him, and she continued to laugh at him, saying now and then, "Oh, my god", and "too much", shaking her head, while he dressed. When he looked again, she was masturbating herself with two hands between her legs, as he tied his laces.

No Prayer

Becker had a stiff Old Crow straight from the bottle in the motel and sang to himself, "Becker the brave, Becker the free."

He realized it had been a dumb thing for him to have suggested assistance from Coca-Cola. Terri would not have considered that acceptable.

Anyhow, he didn't think Sam would come at it. Sam believed in will, pep, and grit.

Somehow she didn't seem as crazy as she came on.

No prayer came to mind.

Coincidence: Non-negotiable Experience

"We have with us tonight, as my guest, a visitor all the way from Atlantic City, Georgia, from the Coca-Cola Company."

"Atlanta, Georgia," Becker corrected, with a good-big smile.

"As you were Fellows, 'Atlanta, Georgia'."

The Rotarians clapped.

Becker was again introduced to yet another Rotary Club. He saw Rotarians rather as those who had the treasure he was after. But they were the Barons—not the Princes. It worried him that they had treasure but didn't know how to eat well.

Where is Rotary going?

Rotary is going to lunch—to a cheap lunch.

The other thing he objected to was that in every damned town he visited and fell in with Rotarians—the local bottler in this case—they took him to the meeting . . . never invited him . . . never gave him an out. . . . They *took* him.

"My daughter Terri is at present working in your city

office," Rotarian T. George McDowell—Classification: Catering—said, introducing himself across the table, half standing, napkin under chin, arm outstretched. Becker didn't like coincidences, because they were an imposition, an infringement of the straightforward, a breakdown of the expected. They had the bad odour of the supernatural about them. Coincidence led nowhere. Where do you go, what do you do with coincidence? It was what Becker called non-negotiable experience.

But strictly this was no coincidence. It was no surprise. "Pleased to meet you, sir. Terri mentioned you were in business hereabouts. I meant to get around to calling."

Becker had hoped to ride his itinerary in and out of the fibro town without so much as a glance towards T. George McDowell.

"She shouldn't be working in an office," McDowell said. "We put her through art school—has just thrown that aside—wasted it."

McDowell showed concern about his daughter, then injury, and then, placing a hand on Becker's arm, changed to smiling, became outgoing. "I love Americans. Both my wife and I love Americans."

"That sounds too generous a statement," Becker said. "You must have to make many allowances for us."

"Not at all. I and my wife love you all. How many times would you say I'd been to the States, at a guess?"

Yet more guessing.

"You travel a good deal?" he rejoined.

"I've been to the States now seventeen times." McDowell sat there, travel-proud.

"You must have a fascination for our country."

"You know what I admire about Americans?"

Becker looked at him, resisting a no and resisting the guess.

"I admire your mental tidiness."

McDowell invited Becker back for a drink after the meeting. "Can't have you going back to some miserable motel room. Not that I'm saying the accommodation in this town is bad, and anyhow I was once in the same trade."

Becker wondered how he could fit himself into the McDowell house, so much carpet, so much bric-à-brac, so many pieces of furniture, so many clocks, so many standard lamps, so many travel souvenirs, so many barometers, pianos, and palms.

"The house is too large for the wife and me now that the children have flown the nest."

His wife was in bed with a backache.

"What will it be?"

They sat with a drink.

"My first trip to the States was to the St Louis Rotary Convention of 1923, with my father. I wasn't a Rotarian myself, but joined Rotary as soon as we could get it going."

"That's a fine record."

Of what?

"That Convention, oh it was really something. The pageant at the Coliseum, corner of Jefferson and Washington streets."

"You remember the streets?"

"Not bad for an old fellow. How is it I can remember the address of the St Louis Coliseum from 1923, but I forget the name of someone I met ten minutes ago? Why is that?"

"It's an often remarked characteristic of later years, sir."

"I remember the flowers—the Rotary Garden of Nations. And they had young girls and boy scouts, and the Rotary Band and the singing of a choir—the Italian Choir of St Louis. Funny that, don't know why an 'Italian' choir. Do you know St Louis at all?"

"No, sir, I'm afraid I don't." Becker shook his head, readying himself to be outknowledged on the United States.

"There it was, in this vast auditorium, massed humanity. How many delegates and observers attended the convention, would you say at a guess?"

"No, sir."

". . . that's with wives, how many?"

"No, I really have little idea."

"Six thousand—nearly seven thousand—and this was Rotary in 1923."

Becker moved his head, impressed, liking a good crowd.

"It was almost pitch-black when we went in. The light gradually brightened at each part of the opening ceremony until the whole spectacle ended in a display of electric light. Now, at the beginning, there was the sound of a trumpet. The sound of a single trumpet in a black auditorium."

McDowell made a trumpeting action and imitated the sound of a trumpet.

"A spotlight then revealed a single figure up there on this long flight of stairs—I think, if I remember, it was meant to be Columbia—standing on top of these stairs. The stairs were covered with green carpet leading to a terrace filled with pot-plants. We had the chorus of welcome sung by the choir—this Italian choir. Then a shrill whistle brought the boy scouts into the hall through the audience, and each bore a flag of the nations represented in Rotary."

"It must have been truly impressive," said Becker from behind his empty glass, thinking especially of the enigmatic spaghetti choir.

"Oh, that was just the beginning. Another fanfare."

McDowell again made the trumpeting action and the imitated sound of a trumpet.

"Another fanfare and from the top of the terrace, in sets of four, trooped twenty-eight girls, representing the twenty-eight nations of Rotary. All dressed in those classical robes and each wearing a band of flowers around their head—they represented the national flowers of the twenty-eight nations in Rotary, Australia included."

"Twenty-eight."

"Twenty-eight, each girl being one of those nations. They carried on their shoulders a huge garland, like a rope, which they hauled down to the main stage and then presented a dance. This was a salute to the visiting nations and an expression of their joy and exhilaration at being present at such a gathering. At the end of the dance the maidens—girls—went back up the stairs to the terrace and their garland was twined among the flags, the flags which the boy scouts had carried up. Can you picture that?"

"Yes, sir, you certainly remember it. More trumpets?"

"No, no more trumpet. This time, instead, the strains of the triumphal march of *Aida*. The rope of flowers was drawn to the top of a gold flagpole now—with your flag, the Stars and Stripes. This was the main feature of the spectacle, and at the same time a huge Rotary Wheel in gold and blue—Rotary colours—glittering, was lit up, twenty feet above our heads. Can you imagine it?"

"Your description, sir, is vivid."

"John Henry Lyons—I think, if I remember, he was from Tacoma, Washington—led the singing. Do you know Tacoma?"

"No, sir, I'm afraid not."

"I've been there, have been to the States now seventeen times. But I've told you that. John Henry Lyons from Tacoma led the singing. We sang 'The Star-spangled Banner,' 'God Save the King', 'America', 'Old Black Joe'—we had song books, of course—but I have never heard men sing out like that since."

"It must have been some occasion."

With a mustering of fervour, McDowell said, "I have never seen anything like it in my life. It has never been equalled in my experience."

McDowell sat there, back among the fanfares and the dancing maidens and the boy scouts.

Then he returned, became the host, rose to fix drinks—but again, paused, mid flight, both empty glasses in his hands, before the ice-bucket, finding the return from 1923 difficult.

"Rotary," McDowell said holding onto the word, "Rotary is my religion", re-engaging, putting down the glasses and going on with getting the drinks. "I hope you don't find that sacrilegious, me saying that, but Rotary has guided my every adult act," McDowell said.

"Oh no . . . no, sir."

"I'm not the churchgoing type, but I am an ethical man and I believe there is a Great Chairman in the Other Country which is the destination of us all."

Mortality was never far from Becker. Becker, replenished by

his drink, wanting to ask about the poor food Rotary ate, and about the treasure promised by Consistent Effort, said instead, "I have never been in one place long enough to join."

"I often say that there is no need to be in a club to live by the principles of Rotary. What we need is not more men in Rotary, but more Rotary in men."

Then McDowell mused, "It has guided the raising of my family. Now take the family. There is good authority, you probably know, for the proposition that a child owes no natural affection to the parents, that such affection will, however, result from kind treatment, companionship, and studied care. The sacredness and survival of the family, I argue, is largely dependent on the environment of Fellowship that is made around it. That's what Rotary and life are about. Complexes cannot live in the Rotary Home. Do you agree?"

Becker scratched around in the remnants of Course 231, Social Psychology. "Complexes, sir, I don't fully follow."

"A complex is when people aggravate their differences, while Fellowship is generally interpreted as a development of the principles on which there can be agreement. One is the seeking of conflict: the other, harmony."

"I follow."

Again McDowell slipped in reverie.

Becker slugged down the drink.

McDowell came up out of the reverie, saying, "What is your honest opinion of my daughter Terri?" A darkness of trouble about his face.

"I really don't know her that well. I spend so little time at the main office."

Two hands masturbating between her legs.

"We haven't seen her for a year." The darkness blackened and without comment McDowell rose, left the room, and returned with a letter.

"I want you to read this. Tell me what you think of a daughter who'd write this to her father."

"Really, sir, I don't think it's my place."

"Go on, I'd like your opinion. I'd like an American

approach." McDowell shook the letter at him in the agitated way of the elderly.

He knew the contents of the letter. He knew no response to the contents. He was thinking of the wording of a response and not reading the letter, he saw it all there in key words from the night in the bedroom under the Archfiend in Goat Form. A loud, blurred letter written with a felt-tipped pen. He saw the words: shaven head, castration, lice, methedrine, a pit of snakes, your cursed daughter.

You didn't need a Soc. Psy. 231 to know it was the letter of a speed freak screaming to her father.

"Really, sir, I don't think it's my place to comment. . . ."

Two hands masturbating between her legs.

"Please, I'd be grateful for any comment. So difficult to seek advice in this town. About this sort of thing."

He guessed McDowell wanted to be confirmed in his judgement. Becker returned to the letter, pretending again to read, and then said, "I guess, sir, it's part of her search."

McDowell didn't acknowledge this, but said, "Do you read the *Reader's Digest*?"

"Yes, sir, I do."

"I like the positive American approach of the *Digest*. It's the only thing I have to go by. This drug thing comes stealing into the home. Remember also that it is not the behaviour of a teenager. Terri's no child, she's nearly thirty." McDowell was grimly bewildered. "She was nurtured in the good fellowship and ethics of this home. I can only put it down to the city life and the company of artistic types."

Becker had not realized that Terri was nearly thirty. Some search. Some of us, he guessed, were looking for more than others. Take himself, for instance.

Becker handed back the letter. The apple is said to fall not far from the tree. But in this case it seemed to.

"Her search, did you say?" McDowell seemed to have just caught up with that, or to have gone back for it. He was having trouble with it, too. "You must stay the night."

"Thank you, sir, but, no, I have luggage at the motel, and I'd like to return there."

"Why, mother would be very hurt indeed if you didn't stay."

"Really, sir, I'd prefer. . . ."

Becker stood up.

McDowell stressed the invitation, the insistent host, the contest of politeness.

"After all, you've been of such good counsel."

"Please, sir, I wish to return to my motel, if you would excuse me."

In the car McDowell laughed again heartily, and said, "I put a strong case, but always remember this, there are three sides to every question—your side, the other fellow's side and the Right Side", and laughed.

Becker was not clear in his own mind to what, if anything, this related.

The Telephone As Bolas

All right then, it was a transactional world. Becker had learned that early enough. One good turn deserved another, a little kindness will be returned a thousandfold. Sam was fond of saying, "Every conversation is a transaction: every meeting is a deal." Well, Sam, what was the trade tonight, what did I give, what did I get?

The motel room was a comfort, to be sure. Not that he was retreating from L-I-F-E, no, sir, not by a dandy long shot. He was still ready to get out and dig for the treasure. But he couldn't see why he should have been selected tonight in this fibro town to receive the ass-pains of Rotarian T. George McDowell and his errant daughter.

A bourbon with ice. Fire and ice. I think I know enough of hate/ to say that for destruction ice/ is also great/ and would suffice.

Becker was not adverse to poetry or to jazz music. He sometimes wondered if this did not soft-edge him, as it were in business. Together with too open and too honest a disposition. Why don't I look like a bastard? Why don't I look like Lee Marvin? Please, God, make me look like Lee Marvin.

Motels. A clean, safe passageway around the world. He

could be in Manitoba. Or good old Atlanta. The joy of standardization. All he asked of his little old hunk of life, for today, was the standard five-star motel. Tomorrow he might ask a castle.

The telephone rang, causing Becker to drop his bourbon.

Ah, shit.

Who in damnation!

Damn you, Sam.

He heard the plug of connection. The telephonist said long-distance person-to-person, "Mr Becker?"

"Yes, this is he."

He heard the wires, saw them stretching along the coast of this fibro nation. He saw the wires stringing him together with someone—a bolas—against his preference— the authoritarian telephone. He watched the mute whites and greys of the television, awaiting the intrusion of the call to bring him stumbling down.

"Hullo, hullo, hullo," he said impatiently.

"Hullo—" a girl's voice—"it's me, Terri."

Terri.

"Jesus! What is this? I've just this moment came from your father's house and how you're busting in down the line."

Becker checked the anger in his voice.

"I want to talk with you and apologize for my uncouth conduct the other night . . . the seduction hassle . . . it wasn't cool, me unloading all that on you."

"Oh hell, forget it."

"What did my father say?"

"Too much. We talked some, we even talked about you. Say, how did you know to get me here, and why this time of night?"

"I made the bookings remember?"

He remembered all right now. From the mit of the father to the mit of the daughter.

"Tell me what my father said."

"Now look, it's very late."

"Did he tell you his daughter was crazy? I bet he didn't."

"He showed me your letter. Yes, as a matter of damned fact."

"He showed you my letter?" Outrage. "Why, that is not fair."

"Look, if you don't mind me saying, I seem to know more about you and your damned family than I want to damned well know."

"He shouldn't have shown you my letter."

Becker began to wonder again. Why? Why me? She went on complaining.

"You can see he doesn't love me, can't you?" Becker took the question, stretched the telephone cable to its limit and, using one hand, poured himself a drink, adding ice.

Becker was in need of a prayer as well as a drink.

Here we go. "No, I don't think he loves you. Not in the way you mean."

Rotary love, maybe? He didn't bother to mention it.

Terri went silent. The line was empty of voice.

"How can you say that?" she came back.

"You asked me—I told you."

Again silence. He could hear a drumming on the line. Wind? God's impatient fingers?

"No one has ever said that before. Everyone said I wasn't being fair to him."

"Well, you asked me. That's the way I see it." Becker sipped his drink, watching the TV picture from the corner of his eye.

"At least you're straightforward."

"I'm going now. I have a big day."

"Selling Coca-Cola." Her voice, returning to normal, was good-natured, but had a derisive edge.

Becker had met derision before. Becker knew about derision.

"Yes, goddam it, doing my simple self-appointed task of selling the best damned soft drink in the world, the best damned way I know how."

Becker believed, among other things, in prowess and the pursuit of excellence.

150

THE PRESIDENT OF THE UNITED STATES ADDRESSING THE CONVENTION, THURSDAY, JUNE 21

The Creed

•

Suggested Creed for New South Wales Country Schools, adapted by T. George McDowell from that used by the Queensland Department of Public Instruction.

I believe in an independent and locally owned agriculture and town commerce; a soil that shall grower richer rather than poorer year by year; a town that shall grow richer in amenity year by year.

I believe the measure of a day's work is tiredness.

I believe a clean farm and a clean town are as important as a clean conscience.

I believe that self-employment is the highest goal for any person.

I believe in the special inspiration which comes from working in the daily sight of nature.

I believe the interests of the townfolk and farmfolk are mutual.

I believe the interests of the skilled man and the employer of skills are mutual.

I believe that every piece of goods I help to manufacture or grow represents part of myself when it goes out into the world.

I believe that life is of two parts, the Private and the Communal, and that the private shall be beyond the reach of the State and that the communal shall be shared.

I believe that the town and the farm are a mutual entity, entitled to run its own affairs.

I believe the only just and manageable government is Local Government, where those who govern are known to the governed.

The Creed was not adopted by the Department of Education up in Sydney. They gave as the ostensible reason that it was "too long".

GWENTH McDOWELL'S STATEMENT CONCERNING HER SISTER, TERESA McDOWELL, JUNE 1969

My name is Gwenth Mary McDowell, I am 36 years of
age and I reside at Unit 6, 221 Penrose Avenue,
Double Bay. I am a single woman. My occupation is
Headmistress (primary). You ask me if there is
anything I can say which may help you with the
psychiatric treatment of my sister, Terri - Teresa.
From what you tell me, I understand that she does
not admit that there is anything wrong and has not
sought assistance voluntarily, which makes your task
so much the harder.

I have not seen my sister for a number of years
(except for one recent meeting), as she has cut off
relations with her family and also because
circumstance, and her way of life, have taken us in
opposite directions. There is a six-year age
difference, as well. No, I do not wish to place any
importance on the age difference. There are many
girls of her age and younger with whom I can speak
as equals. Contrary to the talk in newspapers,
people do not change that much, and there is, in my
experience, no generation gap. It is more that some
people, irrespective of age, seem to go in different
directions - as if there were, in fact, two
distinctly different sorts of humans. Sadly, I am
being forced daily to this view. When you look at
issues such as abortion, sex, and morality generally,
there seem to be just different types of human
beings and all the argument in the world won't
change it. Or so it would seem. As a Christian I am
unwilling to accept that some people are beyond
redemption, but it is difficult not to. I sometimes
feel that an island, say Tasmania, should be set
aside for those who do not want to accept things.

Terri has no religion and may even, in fact,
be, in my opinion, a type of "witch". I know that
this is terribly ~~old-fashioned~~ unclinical (or maybe
not?). What I mean is that she may be
psychologically ~~evil~~ maladjusted, committed to
harming herself and others, though not necessarily

with intention but because of something over which
she had no control, and certainly, I'm afraid,
something which is irreversible. I have done two
years' psychology at the University of New England
and have, of course, read widely in educational
psychology, so I do not speak entirely as a layman.

In our family my mother was the strong person
and a religious woman. Evidence of Teresa's born
antipathy to God was shown early as a child when she
refused to attend Sunday-School or Church. I
remember clearly Terri saying that church
"suffocated" her. My father is not what you would
call a religious man, but I do not want that recorded
against him. He was, in his own way, ethical. But,
of course, Good Works alone is not enough.

We were brought up to love animals, and our
father provided us during childhood with almost a
farmyard of animals. He thought it educational and
as a way of giving us an appreciation of nature. I
believe these views he took from the philosopher
Elbert Hubbard. Despite this, our father was very
much a man of affairs and not particularly spiritual.
Maybe, though, if this love of animals could be
reawakened in her, she might find her way out of the
morass. We not only cared for the animals, and thus
learned a great deal of biology, my sister also
sketched the animals in various poses. Maybe she was
confronted with animal-sex biology too soon. She has
some talent as a sketcher, but in my opinion will
never be an artist. I suppose she has not told you
that she failed to complete Art School?

I raise the next subject because it is a
clinical matter which you, as a social worker, will
understand. She was mortified, I remember, by her
first menstrual period and tried to conceal it from
my mother. She was also disturbed by her breast
development. It was as if she hated womanhood and
wanted somehow to cling to her childhood. As if she
were not willing to leave childhood. But her
embarrassment, or whatever, about her body did not
last long and she soon became known as a flirt (and

worse). I remember another thing about her body which she confided to me. She had one day been examining herself in my mother's mirror and I discovered, by holding a second mirror, that her head, she thought, was badly misshapen. She said she had believed this for a number of years until she realized that, in fact, the two mirrors had caused an optical distortion. But even in recent years she said she has to go to the mirror to check again.

I must say this melodramatic little story of her imaginary deformity did not stop her seeking constantly the attention of boys (and men). In some ways, though I am loath to criticise them, our parents were remiss in the subject of sex education. This did not matter in my case, because I had other interests. As a ~~teacher~~ educationalist, in the course of my duties, I have had to assess a number of books on sexual education and would say that the whole problem seems how to be realistic and frank without being evocative and stimulating. I don't know how one overcomes this problem.

To return to my sister's psychiatric problems. We had a comfortable childhood, although our father had a policy that every penny had to be earned by some completed task. My sister rebelled against this. I remember she once found a mention of a ~~savage~~ primitive tribe, where the status of people in the tribe was measured by their extravagance. I remember her bringing this up at the dinner table. Throwing it at my father.

I do not know if this sounds simple-minded, but I believe her dabbling in drugs was a search for delight. An attempt to find delight the effortless way. The delights of life, as you must know being a social worker, are not that easily found. I myself have found some satisfaction through working with children and the administration of the school, but I would not say that I had found delight, or experienced "the delights of life". I do not complain and do not go seeking this through drugs. Unlike my sister, I do not see it as some sort of

Right. I certainly no longer believe it necessary for a person to experience <u>everything</u> in life. Even if one tried to go through life "using the senses 100 per cent", it is not always possible to do so. "Using the senses 100 per cent", you may recognize is one of her favourite expressions (or used to be). She was very taken with the idea of sensation through the nervous system, and this again may have attributed to her interest in drugs. I myself have opted, I suppose, for the reasonable use of one or two of my senses and experiencing life through the Holy Spirit.

Her life is a profound disappointment to her, I suspect. She has not given due weight to the spiritual (as did my mother) or, on the other hand, to community or professional values (as did my father). She leads a disappointed life because she thought the nervous system could provide everything, be it alcohol, speeding in cars, sex, and at one time, Yoga. And another thing, she thought at one time that it was desperately important to surround herself with the "right" objects, shapes, gardens, and the "right"-sized rooms even, and she spent far too much time and money doing this. She often said, in the times when we were still seeing each other occasionally, that people could make themselves mentally ill by not having the right surroundings. This is sadly ironic. She constantly changed her address in search of the perfect place to live. She was really a gypsy - a gypsy in this, and in other ways.

Where does a young person get such ideas? How do such ideas get into circulation and reach even those protected from such ideas? Why do some ideas grab a hold on some people and not others?

She says every object sends out its own message, which beats incessantly into the brain.

I suppose it's all what is called reaction. Certainly our family did not go about emphasizing the carnal and sensuous.

I do not believe that Teresa likes being alive.

I don't think she likes it very much at all and
hence her constant attempts to alter her life. She
would try anything which took hold of her senses
"100 per cent". Even as a child she would say things
like "I hate life". As if she expected to "like"
life, as if it were a person or an animal. This is a
very wrong perspective, it seems to me. She could
never accept life as a vale of tears.

As a child she was befriended by an old man, an
eccentric, in the town. They were what you might
call "natural friends". I suppose, later, they had
art in common. He was always lending her art
magazines from abroad. He used to call himself
various things from time to time. Once for some time
he was a Dadaist, whatever they may be when they are
at home. It was always thought that he had a degree
from some university or other, but when he died it
was found that this was not so.

It is revealing that these "sorts" of people
always find each other, even in a normal healthy
town.

She often said she could not "learn properly".
She was not dull, nor did she have any obvious
defect, such as hearing. She could not, though,
listen straight and would always get instructions
mixed up, as if, at times, to annoy. It is an
educational problem which should be given more
attention. I think she was overimpressed with life
and its immensity and thought it offered more than,
in fact, life does.

I know all this is probably very revealing
about me. These things always are, but that can't be
helped. Really, there is no explanation for her
conduct. I came from the same family and it was a
very decent childhood. Apart from the death of one
of our sisters, the family has suffered no real
tragedies, suffered no hard times, and not faced
scandal. I don't know if what I've told you is of
any use. I hope that you are able to do something
for her, but I very much doubt it.

The Enterprising Spirit of the Anglo~Saxon Race

HAT next bright morning he called around to the motel to collect Becker and take him to the Lookout—this visiting American he'd met at Rotary the previous night and who knew his daughter Terri in the city.

The American was bemused.

"No," he said to this Becker, "you must see our Points of Historical Interest."

He liked visitors. They filled the time he had, it seemed, these days.

"After all we are, or I was, in the same business, Mr Becker. I was making soft drinks before you were born. Now, of course, retired. Would you believe there were independent cordial-makers in every country town before you chaps came along with your Proprietary lines—Coca-Cola, Jusfrute, Schweppes. Still that's Progress, I suppose."

> I suppose. That's Progress. How you believe in something and it changes like a stick into a snake. Cherished beliefs turn and bite you. Competition. Good for the winner, bad for the loser. And always more losers than winners. That was why people became socialists. Socialism was a system for losers. But for the life of him he couldn't see whether he'd won or lost now, now that it was the final round. Some words were only made clear by the events that arose and followed in and around and behind the word.

"Situations and people's subsequent behaviour make the meaning of some words clear," he said.

"Sorry, sir?"

"Just thinking aloud. No matter."

School of Arts—Tap-dancing, Tues., Thurs., Sat.

"That was where the Science Club used to meet before the war. These days they use it for Housie—the Catholics. I suppose we have the answer to everything now. This has always been a brick town. Weatherboard towns don't trust themselves. I've always said a brick building was a statement of faith."

"Brick, sir???"

Street Light, Weathered-grey Ironbark Blackened with Creosote at the Base

"Believe it nor not, that's our first street light—still standing. Not that it is a Point of Historical Interest. I just mention that in passing. I can remember when it was our only street light. It was a carbide light, before I moved a motion that we have a row of electric lights in the street run off the generator from sunset to midnight, except on moonlight nights—we were a bit tight, that council. I made one of the speeches on Switch-on Night from the back of Carberry's Fiat motor-lorry. . . .

> "How do we get up on the lorry, Henry! Didn't anyone think of steps? What about the Ladies? A butter-box or something! Do I always have to think of everything myself?"

"We had a potted palm on the lorry and a table draped with the Australian flag. Coloured lights. I have always said Australians don't know how to put on a Show—have a proper ceremony. I was telling you last night about the St Louis Rotary Convention. Now, you Americans, you people know how to put on a Show."

"Yes, sir, you did tell me."

> "Electricity is used extensively in America and Europe, and seven towns now have electricity in New South Wales alone. The approach to this town could be a White Way of Electricity—a proclamation of this town's belief in the Scientific Future. No city parliamentarians came. Some of the locals were peeved. I was not. Towns should be masters of their own affairs.
>
> I have always avoided bowing and curtsying to politicians, which is not to say anything against Harry Bate."

"Towns should be masters of their own affairs and powers unto themselves. I have always avoided this bowing and scraping that goes on with city parliamentarians. I remember thinking at the time that electricity power and its conveniences might equalize the country and the city and keep the young from leaving the town. We failed to keep our young. My two daughters have gone."

"There were those opposed to the spending of the £8000. Council could go too far and ride the good horse called Good Times into the ground. There were those on council who would always have you budget for bad times. I have always budgeted for better time ahead."

"Ironbark poles—all ironbark poles and many still standing."

"An unnatural extending of the daylight. 'The moon and the stars are good enough for God,' Old Holdstein, the Lutheran said. We all grinned behind our hand and winked at each other."

"One old chap I remember said that it was extending daylight unnaturally. Most people, he said, didn't want to be moving about at night. But we are go-ahead down this part."

"'You are living in the unscientific past, Mr Holdstein,' I said. 'And you, George McDowell, are an arrogant man, dazzled by mechanical fabrications and unable to have proper fear of their implications.' The others were having a bit of a laugh behind their hand."

"I replied that we have to go where Science takes us. That's the destiny of our Times. He said that he knew very well where Science was taking us."

"Do you mind if I smoke, sir?"

"No, by all means."

He pulled out the ashtray for the American. "I myself have never smoked and did not take alcohol until I was fifty. Both

167

my daughters smoke, I don't know why. I always believed though, privately, that I could become a heavy drinker if I ever had let myself go."

Tutman's Ice Works—"Safe and Pure"—Two Shillings in the Slot

"Now there's an interesting story. My childhood friend, the late James Tutman, built that ice works and it's still going. He was a pioneer of ice-making in this country. First to make block ice, or one of the first. I once predicted that it was finished. Now his son's put ice in plastic bags for service stations and hotels."

> I show James the advertisement from Popular Mechanics for the Tyrell Institute Formula, and we agree to write away for it and try it. It says that it will "magnify your energy, sharpen your brain to razor edge and put a sparkle in your eye". I tell James that we get no answer to our letter, but, in fact, we do and I take the powder but do not tell James. I do not want to share the secret. I should not have done that. I'm sorry, James. I'm sorry. It did not work anyhow. I felt no different.

"We were great friends and business associates and fellow Rotarians. Do you know what my greatest mistake was?"

"No, sir. What was your greatest mistake?"

"I decided against going into ice-cream manufacturing. The coast is ideally suited. Milk, butter, cheese. I decided against ice-cream. Why? I thought domestic refrigeration would spell the end to commercial ice-cream. I thought every woman would make ice-cream in her home. I was wrong. Throughout my life I have underestimated the laziness, lack of initiative, lack of resourcefulness of the human race."

"H. L. Mencken once said, sir, that no one has ever gone broke underestimating the public taste."

> On the balance, things are for the best rather than for the worse. "Where is the proof of

that?" I ask Teacher. "Sit down, George,
and get on with your work."
"Where is the proof?"
"Don't be insolent, George."
Sit down.
Sit down.
I wanted it to be proved, I wanted it to be
true.

Dr Trenbow's Former Residence with Wireless Aerial

"Am I boring you with all this talk of the old days?"

"No, not at all. But sooner or later I have to get on with my
calls."

"That stone residence is where old Dr Trenbow lived.
He, too, was an advanced thinker. He had the first wireless
set in this town and formed a Radio Listening-in Club. It was
in 1924 when F. P. Naylor, representing the Associated
Radio Company of Australia, visited this town.

> F. P. Naylor rises to speak. "It is with great
> pleasure that I come here this evening to
> address your listening-in experiment or-
> ganized by your Science Club. For those of
> you new to wireless the method of use is as
> follows: the family gathers around a table on
> which the wireless receiving apparatus is
> placed. A selective switch is turned—this
> ebonite knob—to get the correct strength of
> sound, this other ebonite knob is turned. The
> best artists in the city travel through the
> ether at 186,000 miles per second. thus
> annihilating distance. The apparatus literally
> takes the broadcast programme 'out of the
> air'. For family listening a trumpet is used to
> distribute the sound equally up to a distance
> of 200 yards. For private listening the ear
> receiver is used." Dr Trenbow and I had
> spent the afternoon rigging up the aerial
> from the chimney to the pine-tree. The doctor

169

had purchased a Burgusphone wireless receiver. Thus annihilating distance.

"The wireless annihilated distance. I'll tell you a funny thing. They used to say that until we had wireless, this town was always about ten minutes behind the world. The town clock was always slow by about ten minutes. Every time someone went up to the city, they found their watch slow. When wireless came, we could set the clock by that."

"That's intriguing, sir."

McDowell's Cordials and Aerated Waters—Tru-frute Flavours —Now Demolished Except for the Brick Front which Still Stands

"I built that factory in 1925, lived in it until I married. Get out, we'll have a look around. You'll be interested, being in the soft-drink business, yourself."

> The Business.
> Business Card.
> Letterhead.
> Printed Invoice.
> Painted Sign.
> Printed Label.
> Advertisements.
> All bearing my name. A person becomes a business entity. An address. A telephone number. A letterhead. There was something fine about it. Something of a special pleasure in a letterhead. A registered business name. The Eckersley Carbonator will be here on Tuesday.

"This is where the Eckersley Carbonator was— over here— and the Progressive bottle-washing machine here. And this here was my office, this slab here was my office."

> My office.
> And these are my tears and this is my aching heart. This was my office and this was my factory. I didn't sell my factory: I sold my works and days.

Economic factors and economy of scale.
"Economic factors and economies of scale. That was where the men's shower was."

Where are the men? What is the future of the country town. We could all live in a single skyscraper. One town in. a single building instead of spreading houses over good acres. Soon, anyhow, the town will be nothing more than a refrigerated outlet for frozen merchandise from the city. The country merchant and the country manufacturer are disappearing.

"Soon towns will be just refrigerated outlets for frozen products made for us god-knows-where by people we've never met. Soon we won't even bake our own daily bread."

Tears.

Tears.

"Morning, George, sentimentalizing again, I see."

Sentimental George? Yes, he was a very sentimental person. Ben Backhouse, queer fish. A good town editor. Stuck by the town.

"Our editor, Ben Backhouse, this is Mr Becker from the United States."

Local papers disappearing. Owned by people you never see. People you can't argue with in the street, can't put a case to. This Max Newton. What happened to Frank Hanley, always working here on some paper on the coast?

"Ben, whatever happened to Frank Hanley?"

"Can't remember, George."

"What happened to Boot? I met Boot once with my father. He had the paper at Tilba and then Cobargo."

"That's a long way back, George."

Time. George. My second daughter died of pleurisy. Wouldn't happen now. I placed an advertisement in the local paper thanking the nurses at the Cottage Hospital and thanking

Dr Trenbow. Don't see that now. I own all
the shops in the arcade.

"I own all the shops in the arcade, which was my idea. How
many towns do you know that have an arcade? But it's not
the same, not the same as being a manufacturer. Why, I'm
just a collector of rents now."

"You've done very nicely, George. No one is going to listen
to your whingeing."

"I was telling Mr Becker that I was in soft drinks myself
until two years ago. No one to take over things. No son. Of
course, I'm a rich man. My eldest daughter has done very
well—a headmistress. I often ask myself these questions . . . ."

What questions?
I once had plans for a political party of
Makers and Growers. This country is run by
financiers, real-estate men, trade unionists,
and public servants—who all make nothing.
I was quite a reader. I was once quite a
philosopher in my own way, and a world
traveller.

"In my own way I was once quite a philosopher. You'd
agree with that, Ben?"

"Oh yes, George, you were."

"I have always said the small town is the answer to our
problems. We will one day have to return to the small town.
I was against *small-mindedness*, but always for *small towns*.
It's not how many square miles in a country that makes it
great: it's how many square people. I see, only recently, a
young fellow from the university agreed with me about the
towns. He said the future is in small communities. I cut the
piece out. His name was McGregor. Or was it Craig. I held
high hopes for the country way of life, Ben. You'd agree with
that. I once wrote the Creed. Do you remember the Creed,
Ben? You printed it. The point of ever larger cities eludes me.
This is where the men's showers were, where I'm sitting now."

Where are the men?
Triple-filtered water was the answer to
impurities in the local supply. I didn't use

172

Blue Ark essence for many years. Made everything myself. All my drinks were 15 parts pure fruit juice. No one noticed when I stopped doing it myself. People don't basically care. Or appreciate. People have never cared as much as I have. Why was that? No one ever commented. I didn't sell my factory: I sold my works and my days.

"George?"

"Ben. Have you met this American chap from Coca-Cola?"

> It's enough to make you weep. Tears of the out-of-business man.

"Come on, George, you'd better get up."

"What time is it, Ben?"

"Nearly eleven."

"Nearly eleven, and we haven't begun our tour of the Points of Historical Interest. Haven't been to the Lookout. Something could happen yet to make this town go ahead. Remember Dorman Long and Co., and what they did for Moruya. Granite for the Sydney Harbour Bridge."

"Maybe, George. But this town's doing O.K."

> A man fell down a mine-shaft and drank his own blood to stay alive for six days. As a boy I was attacked by a sow, and my nose and right arm were broken. Tutman lost a finger. That chap in the garage at Nowra lost an eye when the car battery exploded. Reeves broke his wrist cranking a car. We all lost something or broke something in those days. Life wasn't as safe as it is now, it seems, looking back.

"Ben, I've seen the flower of this town leave."

"George, come along, I'll drive you home. Here wipe your eyes."

"I'm not crying, Ben. Nothing wrong with my eyes. Why, look, everywhere you look—McDowell Cordial bottles, broken glass. I tell you who I saw the other day. Can't bring his name to my lips. He was with the Coastal Steamship

Company. I think he was on the *Benandra* when it sank on the Moruya Bar. Crying? Yes, I'm crying. Why shouldn't I damn' well cry?"

"George, come on, stand up, old fellow."

"What did we pay for the Lookout? How much did it eventually cost the club?"

"Oh, I don't know, George. It was a long time back. Seven hundred pounds, I think."

"There could have been economies."

> Economies of scale and economic factors, and the events and behaviour and personal feelings behind words revealed by the turn of events.
>
> I never spoke to her again after that one unfaithful act. She pleaded, "But, George, it has never been this way for either of us. We were as we had never been."
>
> "We were like animals, and I do not wish to be that way."
>
> They had become like animals on the dirt floor of the Showground Pavilion. She died, impaled on a burning branch in a bushfire. Going away from the town.

"Will you help me, Mr Becker? Give me a hand, and we'll get George over to the car. Come on, George. Stand up."

> Stand up.
> Stand up.
> The class will sing
> Advance Australia Fair
> Blue Bells of Scotland
> Dear Little Shamrock
> The Song of Australia
> Rule Britannia
> One two three
> George will speak on The Enterprising Spirit of the Anglo-Saxon Race.

I must dig out those accounts. They must be

in a box somewhere.

I never had an experience like it with anyone else before or since. It remains singular and alone.

All right, children,
one, two, three.

In those days one could not afford the risk. You can never be certain. Never trust your memory.

"My recollection, Ben, is that it cost more than £700."

"Give me a hand. Come on, George, over to the car. Steady now, he's quite a weight."

"He seemed to be in good spirits when he called for me at the motel. Obviously the demolished factory and all."

"Come on, George, you can't sit here in the rubble."

"I think, Ben, I'll start again from scratch. It's my view that there'll be a swing back to country-made things. I'll start again from scratch."

"Come on, George. Here wipe your eyes. No one is going to listen to your whingeing. You've done very nicely."

A
COINCIDENTAL
NARRATIVE

An Application for a Film Grant

•

Extract from an Application for a Film Grant for the Film
The Australian of the First Half Century

". . . as the material covers a lengthy time-span, a stylized form of storytelling is employed. Each sequence is, we hope, to be one shot. There is absolutely no cutting within the interview sequences. The documentary footage will be interlaced with the interview sequences. Each sequence will either fade or iris in and out. There will be enough emotive, even perhaps heart-rending, material without building up melodrama by cutting. In the enclosed treatment we list interview 'topics', but the filmed interviews will essentially be ad-libbed . . . ."

FILMING
THE
HATTED
AUSTRALIAN

IT is not my idea.

    We, the film crew, arrive at the football ground:
Director Stewart, Peter Sound, Gary Camera, Continuity
Jane (who is also on with Stewart), Terri Props, etc., Me
Script. But there is no script.

We are looking for an Australian, vintage 1910 or there-
abouts.

We stalk through the crowd draped in equipment, me
hanging back. We are going to pounce on the "subject"—
extract him clean, gut him from his life.

—how about that guy, says Peter Sound, pointing at a
hatted, fifty-year-old.

We look.

—no, says Director Stewart, hardly looking, no.

Peter Sound can never be right. A sound man can never be
right about anything outside Sound. That would be wrong.

—I think *that's* him, I think that's him says Director
Stewart, pitch rising up with enthusiasm.

We all look. A hatted fifty-five-year-old sits on a newspaper
in a synthetic knit shirt, binoculars, smoking a roll-your-own.
He does not wear sunglasses. Stewart had stipulated that he
must not wear sunglasses. The man must be pre-sunglass.
Stewart raises both arms outstretched as if to hold us back
from rushing the man. As if we might startle the man and
send him fleeing into the undergrowth of crowd.

"The Undergrowth People"—a title?

—back, let's get some long shots, candid, just pull in on him.

We stand shooting. I clap it. I feel that just by being there
for any purpose other than football-watching offends the
spirit of the place and interferes with others.

Director Stewart has not revealed his plans in detail. He
has told us he will not fully reveal his plans because he does not
want us leapfrog-thinking him, because he does not want to
bruise the vision with too many inadequate words and minor
misinterpretations (he says that most films are "a multitude
of minor misinterpretations put together with a multitude of
minor compromises", he wants to avoid this), because he
does not want to reduce his vision to something that can be

"explained", because we must learn to follow the *scent* rather than the *plan*, and, with uncharacteristic honesty, he says he has not thought through what he wants.

As for the script, he says we will write the script *after* we have shot the film.

—right, cut, now let's approach him. I will do the talking, says Stewart.

—do we walk in single file? I say.

We approach with all the stealth of a film crew, leads, boxes, clapperboards, clipboard, bumping and breaking all before us.

—excuse us, sir.

The hatted Australian, binoculars to eyes, shifts with fright.

—may I have a word with you? We are a small film unit. We are making a film about football and its followers. We would like to talk with you about it. There is a small payment, of course. We have received a grant from the Federal Government. But we are no big Hollywood company or anything like that.

It is Stewart's ABC voice which he took with him when he left.

—come again mate? says the fifty-five-year-old politely defensive. Is he being sold something? He does not grasp.

Stewart is patient. He explains further.

The man looks at each of us and says:

—oh yeah?

I avoided his gaze. I am not sure whether this means, yes I will do it, or yes I understand, or just a question rolled into a reply.

The man doesn't know the camera is on silent roll. Stewart had patted his head, which is the signal for silent roll.

The Australian in the hat, for want of something better to do with the situation, has gone back to the football, obviously unable to size up the situation, having no stock response for this.

Informally, Stewart squats beside the man and motions to

me to hand him the prepared "dummy" questions: age, place of birth, so on.

Stewart asks him which team he follows, using now a modified voice, used by intellectuals when talking with Real Australians.

—come again, mate, the man says. On cue.

It clearly means, "What are you doing squatting there beside me, asking questions in that phony voice."

The man turns his eyes back to the game, but he is still paying some sort of attention to Stewart.

Continuity Jane throws up her eyebrows at me.

—end of roll, says Gary Camera.

While Gary is reloading the camera, Stewart explains it all again to the man.

—don't think I'm your man, he says.

—come on, it won't take long and there's money in it.

This, I think, will offend his dignity. I think it suggests that he, an Australian, is mercenary. The working people can't be so easily bought, I've been told.

—not my line of work, friend, he says.

Eyes back to the football, binoculars, up, we've lost him. The impassive self-contained Australian. Ah yes.

None of this is my idea. I am embarrassed.

Continuity Jane crouches down.

—oh please, it would help us a lot if you would.

Her voice is the one little girls use with their daddies, and later in public relations.

He looks at her, a different approach, sucks his teeth. The approach I thought was now discredited as sexist.

—nah, not my line, girlie.

—oh please, you'd be so good at it. You're so *right*.

—you're just trying to get around me, he says, winking at Stewart.

Face breaking into girlish smiles, Jane pushes back a wisp of hair from her ingénue face and has to admit she is trying to win him over. So artful.

—please? she pleads.

—what's it all about again? he says, weakened.

She explains this time.

He's buying time, getting the information together in his head, taking in a little more on each repetition, piecing it together.

—tell me if I've got this straight. You (pointing at Jane) want to make a picture about me (points at himself) about what football team I follow and my opinion. Have I got you straight?

—yes, says Jane, turning deferentially to Stewart, who nods vigorously.

What she and Stewart are saying is just not true. I know that much.

The Australian turns back to the football. Considering, he pulls a blade of battered grass from the trodden football ground, makes tooth-picking movements, thinking, thinking.

He turns back to Jane.

—you want to make a picture about me going to the football, right?

—yes.

—can't see the story in that.

He's right.

—about football, the followers, the different teams, she says, making it up.

—you say you're from the government?

—no, we have money from the government, a grant.

—you from TV then.

—no, just doing it for ourselves.

—the government gives you money to make a film about me going to the football?

—yes, Jane says, smiling hard.

—can't for the life of me see the story in that.

What we got the grant for was to make a film about the prejudices, the beliefs, the life-style (especially "life-style", oh yes, the life-style, especially) of the self-contained Australian of this vintage; *The Australian of the First Half Century*, we called it in our submission.

To be fair, I guess that Stewart's way is to begin on familiar ground like football, so that we can break and enter the man's personality.

—just a few questions, Jane says, wheedling.

—suppose it's all right, fire away, but I can tell you now there's no story in me.

He is now the humble man.

Now he's submitted, he becomes immediately embarrassed and uncertain of what he's supposed to do. He has shifted into a limelight which is too bright for his liking but—too late. He is no longer unnoticed.

I clap it. The man is moving about his hands and head, shifting his newspaper mat, ill at ease as all hell.

He answers the dummy questions, trying at the same time to look over Stewart's hand at the written list on the clipboard.

Yes, he played football at school, and then for the town team at Milton, and in the army. He played outside centre. They were the best days of his life. The days of football matches.

He's a bachelor.

—work?

—been many things in my day.

Oh, of course, I think, of course.

—working out at the abattoirs at Homebush just now. Could have been many things. Could have got on.

Lost promise.

—I'm from the South Coast, worked on the coast mainly.

Probably knows my father, Terri says to me.

We finish all the routine questions and Stewart hops about saying, fine, wonderful, that was great.

—what we want, says Stewart, is to come to where you live tomorrow and ask you a few more questions where it's a little quieter. Won't take long.

—not that much to tell, son, that's about it.

He's suspicious.

—would tomorrow afternoon be O.K.?

—never been one for talking.

—please, says Jane.

—really not my line of business.

—you were great, says Jane.

—maybe if it won't take long, got things to do on Sunday.

—it won't take long.

We have projected something like ten shooting days, I don't know what's going on.

It wasn't my idea.

Jane asks if he would like to be paid now or by cheque.

He says now would be all right with him, but it makes no difference one way or another; cheque in the mail would be all right.

Pretended indifference to money.

She pays him twenty-five dollars.

He stares at the money.

—I get twenty-five dollars for answering those questions?

He is pleased, but finds it a bit too far from the ordinary, far enough to suggest that there'd been a mistake. Or that it was illegal.

—that's right.

—what's the catch?

—no catch.

—all right by me. He breaks out in smiles. Says he's in the wrong game.

He becomes uneasy when he has to sign the receipt-release. He makes a motion of reading the form.

He prints his name. Jane has to get him to sign.

He then does it quickly, illegibly, as if to get it out of his consciousness as fast as possible.

—where did you jokers say you were from—TV?

—no we're just film-makers.

—oh yeah, I see.

He doesn't see at all.

In the Station Sedan After Shooting

—I think he's going to be great, says Stewart.

—did you see his face when I gave him the twenty-five bucks? says Jane.

—yes! did you get that, Gary. Did you shoot that? Stewart asks.

Gary Camera says, yes, he got that.

All the "cuts" are phony. The real cuts are by prearranged signal. Most of the filming is done when the "subject" thinks we aren't.

"I want all that stuff, I want all the stuff when he thinks he's not being filmed. How'd he look, Gary? How will he come up?

—he's got a great head, says Gary.

—fine, fine, says Stewart.

—he probably knows my Old Man if he comes from down around Milton, says Terri.

—we might be able to use that, says Stewart.

Day Two

Frederick Victor Turner is a bit drunk when we arrive.

He's a bit aggressive.

He's been "talking to a mate at work", and the mate at work says he should be getting paid a lot more and not to sign anything. He mentions a thousand dollars.

There we are at the doorstep, weighed down with gear.

There goes the signal. We're shooting.

But Jane explains (we decided that she would negotiate difficulties, after her earlier success). We are just learning the film business (not true—we are all professionals), and we are just a little group of struggling beginners, we have only this tiny grant from the government.

—but you said you were from TV. He's truculent.

—no, no, it might get on TV, but it might not. We'll show it at the universities and so on.

—you university students then, he says, seizing on the category.

—well, no, we are just a group of independent film-makers.

—it's not going TV then, he says, disappointment and relief in one.

—maybe we'll sell it, but we are not from a TV station.

Jane then dangles Paul Hogan's name before his eyes.

—thought it was for TV, he says, letting us in, explaining his greed. We troop into his rooms.—I thought it was for TV, but

anyhow you think we might still be in the big money? I'll
give it at go.

If we do make any money, I don't see how he'll get any.

He sits in his arm chair, a big oily, hair-stained arm chair.
We give him a can of beer.

—right, says Stewart, let's start from the beginning—where
were you born and so on.

Slate Four, Aussie, I say, marking it.

—speed, says Gary.

—right, Frederick Victor, start talking.

—you mean, where I was born and so on?

—yes, the camera is rolling, says Stewart. Frederick clears
his throat.

—I was born at a very early age.

We exchange agonized glances. How long has he been
thinking that up.

—cut, says Stewart (a false cut). Now let's start again
Where and when, dates, and places, Frederick.

He begins again.

I was born in Milton, on the South Coast.

"I was born at the foot of the mountain,
taught my first letters in sand."

O Jesus.

—my father was a saddler. I worked around the Shoalhaven
district, milking cows, cutting sleepers, bringing telegraph
poles down the river; my father said I was a ne'er-do-well
because I never learned a trade. Here's something I bet you
never would guess, I sang in the Nowra Musical and Operatic
Society once in *Chu Chin Chow*. I took quite a ribbing, I tell
you, for singing in that operatic society. They said, though, I
had a good voice and with a bit of training and coaching they
said I could have gone on with singing. But I wasn't much of
an actor.

—hold it, Frederick. We want dates and places. Tell us
when.

—will I start again?

—yes, If you want.

> —"I was born at the foot of a mountain,
> taught my first letters in sand."

I was born at Milton in 1918. I worked there for a while. I remember when they cut up Lenin's brain into 31,000 pieces and found he had pyramids, his brain was all pyramid shapes and that was how he got his ideas, his brain was not normal. I was the first watchman allowed to carry a gun outside Sydney. For a while I played in the town band, cornet; after we got electricity the band hall was one of the first to have heaters. I was a volunteer fireman and went to classes about what to do with electricity when there was a fire and it was escaping. Damned scared we were. Some of them wouldn't fight the fire at the garage because of escaping electricity. We got an old Abo drunk once, and he told us where to find Billy Blue's reef up at Yalwal—you could cut solid hunks of gold off it— but we got so drunk ourselves that we'd forgot in the morning. . . .

Back at Jane's Place Later

—it's all so much garbage, it's too static, Jane says.

—no, no, no, says Stewart, no, this is just the warm-up. This guy is good.

—he's an interesting type, I say, he's the sort of person who fills the gaps in the economy. Adaptable, learns new techniques.

—that's what the film is about, says Stewart.

He doesn't mean that. He just says that.

—but you're depriving him of his dignity, Jane bursts out, because he thinks you are making a film about what you've told him. But really you're making it about things you've never told him.

—that's not a film-maker's response, says Stewart sternly. If you feel bad about it you're in the wrong business. He, the subject, has to look after himself. We have to fight with reality to get what we want. It's a battle of wills. We have to attain our objective, regardless. Anyhow, you're the one robbing him of his *dignitas* by not conceding him the ability of looking after himself.

—I'm certainly not conceding him *that*. She laughs.

189

—that's what show business is all about. Right, Gary? says Stewart.

—you find 'em, I shoot 'em, says Gary.

—what a trouper! says Stewart.

Day Three

—well, how goes it Frederick Victor? Ready to make movie history? asks jovial Stewart.

—I've been thinking. I'm not sure I know what you boys are on about.

—just a few questions tonight, Frederick, perhaps a few more tomorrow night.

—but I don't know what you fellows want. I don't think I know what it's all about.

—just sit down and relax.

Stewart goes into more personal history asking for "significant memories".

—once saw an Avro Anson land in a paddock . . . once went to Braidwood to see a demonstration of a new fly-trap, which they said caught 30,000 flies in a week using a piece of bullock's liver and honey . . . never seen so many flies, thick black like tar they were . . . this fellow who made this fly-trap was going to put one for every five hundred acres . . . he reckoned that there'd be no more flies in the country . . . don't know why he didn't go ahead with it. . . .

—entertainment?

—remember going to see Clay's Variety and seeing Nellie Kolle dressed up as a man.

—you liked that, Frederick?

—around the thirties I was great mates with Harry Miller who could get more timber out of a tree than any man I ever knew . . . bloody marvellous he was . . . I worked with him . . . he and me made all the post and rail fences you see up and down the coast. You could go there tomorrow and see them there. . . .

—you made all the fences, eh?

—one day we'd be working away, could be any time of the day, and I'd see Harry just drop his tools and all and walk off

190

without a word . . . I knew what would be up . . . about every two months or so . . . he'd be off on a drunk . . . leaving his tools, everything, just where it was . . . if I wasn't there to pick them up they would've just stayed there till he came back . . . I used to go with him for the first few hours . . . but he'd just drink until he fell down and go on for days, stopping just like he started, and go back to where he'd left off. No one could make a fence like him; he got more timber out of a tree than any man I knew. We must have built hundreds of miles of fences. . . .

Day Four

—right, Frederick Victor, Stewart says.

Fred is ready early. Sitting in his chair, hair done. He's now only too willing to sit in front of the camera to talk about himself. He has discovered film, the ultimate egomaniacal business, where everyone from subject to director feels unnaturally important.

—right, Frederick Victor, tonight is going to be a little different. We've heard all you have to say about the good old days, and how you built the South Coast. Today things are going to be a little different. Today I'm going to talk to you about what our generation thinks of your generation—damn it no—to be specific, what *I* think about *you*.

Stewart hasn't warned us about this. This wasn't how I saw it all going.

—first your attitude to pleasure, Frederick. You could all get drunk, we know that, but did you ever sing? No. Did you ever dance? We know you could tell dirty jokes, but you were never really comfortable with women, women had no place with you and your generation. The bachelor is a sort of hero. You were hung up with sex but could never admit it. Your generation never admitted being wrong, hung up, and you went on to be so damn' self-righteous about every bloody thing, you buggered up your kids.

—ain't got no kids, says Fred aggressively.

—for god's sake, Frederick, I'm talking about your generation, not you particularly. Your generation never could admit its failings, could never examine itself, could never. . . . For instance, Frederick, where do you get your fucks from, tell us how you work things out?

Fred looks across at Jane and Terri protectively.

Stewart, I think, is not that coherent, he is I think playing it off the top of his head.

—it's all right, Frederick, we don't have a double standard like you. We talk the same way to our friends irrespective of whether they're male or female. You treated women despicably.

—hey now, just you mind what you're saying, says Fred.

—your fake toughness, too, you and your generation's gruffness, hiding your ignorance.

—you know what you can do? says Fred. You can piss off, the lot of you. I'm not here to be insulted.

—oh yes, you are. Ho, ho, that's just what you are. Jane was saying only yesterday how you were being deprived of your *dignitas*. Because you haven't got a clue in all hell what's going on. And you didn't have the guts to ask or the nouse to guess.

—go on, piss off, says Fred, getting to his feet, flustered and hurt. Piss off, the lot of you.

He motions with his hand and goes into the other room.

—we'll wait, says Stewart.

We sit around nervously, smoking, drinking, or pacing.

—I might go to the pub, I say.

—you stay. We might need some more probes, barbs. Start feeding me.

He snaps his fingers.

—feed me, questions which sting, he says.

—at least it wasn't static, says Jane.

—bugger off, the lot of you, he yells from the other room. Bugger off.

Stewart gets Peter Sound to hold the mike against the door.

—all right, Fred, stop this prima donna bit and come out. Come on, tell us about how you fought on the Kokoda Trail, tell us about serving with the Eighth Divvy, how you worked on the Burma railway, put the telegraph across Central

Australia, hewed the granite for the Sydney Harbour Bridge, dug the Parkes Swimming Pool during the Depression, was the first person to retread a tyre, built every fence on the South Coast, picked up Chifley's pipe when he dropped it at Bathurst once, shook General Montgomery's hand. . . .

Stewart ran out of questions.

—Christ, take it easy, Stewart, I say.

We sit a bit longer, but Stewart is wrong. Fred doesn't come out.

Day Five

Jane and I go back to reapproach Fred and to pay him his twenty-five dollars for Day Four.

He answers the door.

—can we come in and talk with you, Mr Turner. We're sorry about how things turned out last night.

—where are the others? He is brusque, formal.

—we came around to say we're sorry, says Jane. I nod.

—like to get me hands on that bloody Stewart.

Stewart is crouched with Gary in the hedge with sound gear and a sungun ready to pounce.

As soon as Fred says this, up Stewart and Gary jump, sungun beaming.

—now's your chance, Fred, says Stewart.

Fred sort of laughs with fright. There is a bit of laughing, and we're back in the living-room with Fred the centre of attention and the camera rolling. Good spirits.

To soften him up, we let Terri Props, etc., ask a few questions about the coast where she comes from. She's more nervous on camera than Fred.

—George McDowell! Old T.G.! You his daughter! Go on! Well what-do-you-know! Fancy that! Know him! I used to work for him, probably before you were born. Know him! I used to wash bottles in his bloody cordial factory. He was very particular about that. Well, strike me pink!

—what sort of person was he?

—what sort of person was he? Your father? Old T.G.? Fair, a fair man, but as hard as nails the old T.G. Know his biggest problem? He didn't understand people. Was always rubbing people up the wrong way. One day I remember Tony Larkins got a dreadful dressing down from T.G., a real bawling-out because Tony said something to me about crawling to the boss. Tony was having me on, like. T.G. went for him. Tony and me drank together. But old T.G. overhears Tony say something about me crawling to the boss, because I'd done something or other to make the line work better. Old T.G. heard him and really let fly. And bugger me, but he doesn't give me a raise. For having improved things. But you know what? It was Tony's idea all along. He told me in the pub about the idea to make the line work better and I was just rigging it up! He gets bawled out by T.G. and I get the raise. We laughed ourselves sick in the pub. Your old man, eh! Fancy that!

Stewart lets this go on for a while, although he's not really interested. But Fred likes talking about it, and we obviously need to win him back on side.

We make it an early night.

Day Six

This time Jane prepares Fred.

—you know, Fred, these days we all talk about sex. People these days want to know about how it is with other people and so on. There's more honesty about now. Well, we'd like to talk to you about it.

—sex? But everyone will see me.

—but these days it doesn't matter.

—but Stewart promised no more of that personal stuff.

We are shooting this little exchange, too.

Stewart comes in.

—right, Frederick, stop behaving like an old woman. Let's talk about prostitutes.

Fred is sullen.

—come on, Fred, you've got your twenty-five bucks. Why you're almost in the same business yourself.

—about what?

—come on, Fred, you must have gone to a prostitute once in your life.

—had a friend up in Nowra. We were sort of engaged, I suppose you'd say, but she off and marries this cocky. I was working down the coast; it would have been about the time I was working for young Terri's father. I'm not the marrying kind. I guess if I'd wanted to marry her, I wouldn't have gone down the coast.

—all very interesting, says Stewart, but what do you do for sex on the coast when you're not the marrying kind?

Fred gives a sheepish grin.

—when did you first visit a prostitute, Fred?

—that's a bloody silly question. How would I remember that? Probably in Cairo during the war.

—Jesus, he *was* in the Egyptian campaign, Stewart says, rolling his eyes at us. Turning back to Fred, he says, how old were you?

—twenty something.

—before that it was your courtship. Did you "indulge" while engaged?

—sort of.

—sort of?

—I don't want to talk about her now. She's a respectable woman.

—all right, what about Aboriginal women?

—never an Aboriginal.

—why not? Prejudiced?

—no, I'm not a prejudiced man.

—then why not with an Aboriginal.

—they're a different race and I don't believe in the races mixing.

—that's prejudice.

—it's a bloody fact of life. Old Cocky Calwell was right on this particular issue.

—pure prejudice.

—not in my book, it isn't.

—we must have a look at your "book", Fred. What is it? *Mein Kampf.*

Silence.

—so you've never been with a black woman.

—I might have been with a half-caste.

—only partially prejudiced then. Stewart enjoys his joke.

—tell us what you say when you go to a prostitute.

—say?

—what do you talk to them about. I wouldn't know myself.

—talk?

—what do you ask them, what do you say? Do you talk about the weather?

—do you ask about the price? prompts Jane overeagerly from the sidelines.

The embarrassment is burning me to death.

—yes, Frederick, or do you just take out your prick and put it in their hands and burst into tears.

—how much, he says reluctantly.

—then what. Do you say, "Beautiful weather."

—something like that.

—do you ever ask them to go out with you, try to get to know them better?

He blushes, and is overcome with both the intrusion and some sense of personal misbehaviour.

—go on, tell us, says Stewart, soft, coaxing, confidential.

—might have, once, if I particularly fancied a girl.

—did they ever go out with you, Frederick?

—sometimes they did.

—bullshit. Stewart is hard again.

—a girl in Bega once.

Stewart waits, staring disbelievingly, sternly at Frederick.

—she really fancied me, that sheila. He is losing confidence, his words come out weakly.

—a lot of them won't, you know. Won't go out with you. Scared of their boyfriends.

He says this as unconfident explanation.

—ever hit a woman, Frederick?

I am surprised at this question. Stewart must have sensed something that I didn't.

—no. Frederick is defensive. Not really.

—what do you mean "not really"?

—I hit a whore once.

—for what?

—I forget.

—come on, Fred, you remember.

—I wanted to kiss this girl and she wouldn't let me.

—kiss her? This was a prostitute?

—she wouldn't let me. She said it would make her puke. I hit her then.

We all stare, transfixed. I think even Stewart is caught up. The fifty-five-year-old man, actually hanging his head with embarrassment, the whirring of the camera motor, the crushing silence.

Jane's Place

—fantastic, that was simply fantastic, Stewart is saying, walking around, running his hand through his hair, drinking his drink in gulps.

—we've got enough footage for thirty minutes, I say, hoping we can finish up now.

—we can get more, he says. Old Fred is really opening up.

Day Seven

—well, Frederick Victor, you've made your first one hundred and fifty dollars, coming up for one hundred and seventy-five.

—no more of that stuff like the other night, Stew.

—no, tonight . . . tonight we do politics.

—never been one for politics, Stew. Not a party man, that's a principle of mine. I always vote Labor, but I'm not a party man. It's my firm belief that there should be a party to look after the working man, but that your average working man can't run the country. Do you follow me? What the Labor Party needs is educated men. Like Doc Evatt and Gough—educated men. The working men should pay these people to represent them. Do you follow?

—do you know any political songs? asks Jane, who collects Industrial Songs.

—come off it, Jane, says Stewart impatiently. Sometimes Jane is a pain in the arse.

—what about legalization of homosexuality? What about the poofters, Frederick?

—how do you mean?

—what are your feelings?

—feelings?

—what's your opinion?

Nervous grinning. Fred looks down and then around at us, way down he senses that what he thinks may not be "right" in our eyes. But he hasn't any way of finding out what the "right" answer is that will please Stewart.

—nothing against them. But it does say in the Bible that they should be put to death.

—ah! The Bible. I believe this is the first time you've mentioned the Bible, Frederick. Would you put them to death or in jail?

—if they get caught at it.

—what about brain surgery?

—yeah, the brain or a bit lower. Say, between their legs.

He laughs at his remark and looks around, but stops when he sees no sharing of the joke.

—ever been with a man, Fred?

—come off it.

—what if I was to tell you that Gary there behind the camera and Peter on the sound recorder fuck each other? Would you ring the police?

—you're just having me on.

—no, it's true (Stewart turns), isn't it, boys?

Gary raises a hand of assent, and Peter nods. It is all prearranged.

Fred goes red.

—what people do in private's all right by me, he mumbles.

—you're a weak bastard, Fred. You change your opinions under pressure. Typical.

—a man's entitled to his opinions, says Fred.

—right through the filming, Fred, you've searched around for answers which would "please us". You've twisted and

198

changed your so-called opinions to win approval.

—look, I work for a living. I'm not a pack of bludgers like you lot. From the university or whatever part of the woodwork you crawled out of.

—no, Fred, you have no pride, no opinions.

Stewart acts out disgust and turns away.

—cut, it's all a waste of time, he says to Gary.

This is all prearranged. It's a false cut.

—you can all piss off, for all I care, says Fred.

—look, Fred, your whole generation is servile. You never took your life into your own hands. You were always servile with the boss, with authorities. You never asserted your rights to run this country, to share in profits, to have a place in running factories. You fought willingly in whatever bloody war came along.

Stewart is quite angry. I think he's really disgusted this time.

—the whole point of this film, Fred, is to show the typical Australian—pliable, servile, bigoted . . . dullards.

Frederick is goaded, unexpectedly.

He gets up and gives Stewart a push, telling him to piss off. And then he throws a punch.

Stewart suddenly seems so much bigger than Fred, and actually holds Fred's wrists.

I move in and try to separate them, saying cooling things.

Fred doesn't calm down, he abuses us all and then tries to kick the sound equipment.

I hold him off, while we get the gear together and get out.

Day Eight

We go to see Fred for the final session. Jane, Terri and me front him again. He says he is going to his solicitors about stopping the film. The inevitable "mate at work" has an inevitable "brother in law" who knows all about this sort of thing.

Jane and Terri use their charm and the name of Paul Hogan.

It takes about fifteen minutes of talking, an agreement that there'll be no more politics, sex or insulting remarks. An apology from Stewart, and a promise that we won't use any of the stuff about his sex life. We promise, but, of course, we'll use it.

But as it turns out, there is nothing more to be got from Fred.

He goes back over the same ground. He does show us a reference that Terri's father wrote for him back in the thirties, which says in part, "A first-class type of workman. A man who always leaves his brushes clean, always cuts a piece of timber straight and true, and always drills a 90-degree hole. Most importantly, he is the sort of person who can come up with a good idea."

Fred says it's the oddest reference he ever got.

We take him for a feed and a bellyful of booze at a good restaurant. We do some filming of Fred in the restaurant, talking to the waiter.

Later, back at his place, he sings "Waltzing Matilda" to the camera, but does not know the words.

We rap and sit around having a few last beers.

We learn later that he tries to get it on with Jane while she's in the lavatory.

Jane's Place

Next day Stewart makes Jane tell what happened in the lavatory.

She says it was somewhere between a declaration of love and rape.

Stewart considers going back and confronting him, or getting him to act it out.

Jane will not be in it.

Nor will I.

Gary says that since the homosexual stuff, Fred has avoided him and avoided looking into his eyes.

We sit around telling our favourite Fred Story.

Stewart says,—he came up to me at the end and said, "—well, Stew, you and me mates now? No hard feelings?" I said, "—yes, Fred, you and me is mates now."

South Coast Expressions

•

"Doing the Government Stroke"—from timber-cutting—the non-productive stroke of the crosscut saw—the one that doesn't cut. The unproductive role of government.

"Stay and lick the bastard."

"A hand-round supper."

"A sit-down supper."

"To run into town"—to drive into town.

"They used to nearly live in the sulky"—always out and about. Sulky—a light, two-wheeled, horse-drawn carriage.

"A service car"—a passenger car which travels a set route.

"Up to Town"—up to Sydney

"Making up the coast"—on my way up the coast.

"In business to make money—not friends."

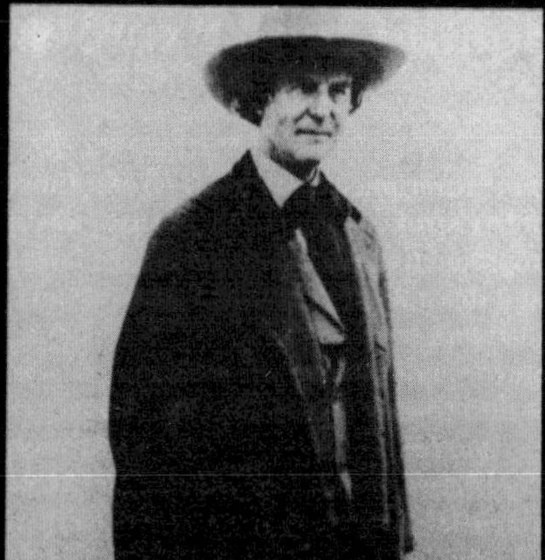

Notes and Acknowledgments

•

1. For those who would like to know a little more about Terri, I refer them to the stories "I Saw a Child for the Three of Us" in *Futility and Other Animals* (Angus and Robertson 1973); Terri and Becker together appear in "Soft Drink and the Distribution of Soft Drink" and "Jesus Said to Watch for 28 Signs" in *The Americans, Baby* (Angus and Robertson 1972); and Becker himself in "The Coca-Cola Kid", "Becker on the Moon" and Becker and the Boys from the Band" also from *The Americans, Baby*. More of Dr Trenbow can be learned from the film "Between the Wars" directed by Michael Thornhill.

2. The story, "The St Louis Rotary Convention 1923, Recalled", also appears in *The Americans, Baby*. I have used it again because it is the starting-point for this book and I ask you to read it again in this new context. It is also one of my favourite stories.

3. I would like to thank my father and mother for their special help with this book.

4. I am also in debt for assistance given by the late Gordon F. Anderson.

5. The book was written partly while on an Australian Council for the Arts Literature Board grant and partly, before receiving the grant, with the financial help of my friends—from the free lunch to the non-

repayable loan—for which I will be permanently
grateful.

6.   "A Black, Black Birth" first appeared in the *Sun-
      Pictorial*, "George McDowell Does the Job" and
      "George McDowell Delivers a Message to General
      Juan Garcia of the Cuban Army" in the *Bulletin*, "The
      End of Ice" was broadcast by the ABC, "The St Louis
      Rotary Convention 1923, Recalled" first appeared in
      Pol, "Rules and Practices for the Overcoming of
      Shyness" in *Hemisphere*, "Tell Churchill T. George
      McDowell Is on His Feet" in *Southerly*, and Gwenth's
      statement in *Cosmopolitan* as "Sister/Sister".

7.   Stephen Knight, Don Anderson, and Sandra Levy
      had that sticky job of giving an "objective" critical
      reaction to the stories in manuscript, one of the most
      delicate services a writer can ask of his friends and I
      thank them for risking it. Edna Wilson and Adrian
      Haber assisted with research.

8.   Although in the stories George McDowell lives in a
      town "somewhere south of Nowra" on the New South
      Wales coast, he and the other main characters are not
      biographical studies of living people.